JUST A GIGOLO
A young man's story of
Berlin in the 1920's

Rosemary Kingsland

Just a Gigolo

Based upon a film
script by Joshua Sinclair

CORGI BOOKS
A DIVISION OF TRANSWORLD PUBLISHERS LTD

JUST A GIGOLO
A CORGI BOOK 0 552 11005 1

First publication in Great Britain

PRINTING HISTORY
Corgi edition printed 1979

Corgi Books are published by Transworld Publishers Ltd,
Century House, 61–63 Uxbridge Road,
Ealing, London, W.5.
Made and printed in Great Britain by
William Collins Sons & Co Ltd, Glasgow

ONE

He had a Fatherland; the others had a Motherland. That was the difference.

"Die with a bullet in you, son," his father, the Colonel, had said. "Die with a bullet in you – it's the only honourable way for a soldier to go."

Uber alles, uber alles, uber alles.

He strutted like a god over the snow, his boots and hair smooth and gleaming, ignoring the shells as they screamed over his head. Heroism was his destiny and his fate lay in the lap of the Gods.

The bleak landscape was black and white and jagged, filled with the broken stumps of trees, gaunt black bicycle frames and cartwheels hanging in space. The shells exploded like red flowers rising in sudden brilliant expansion from the black earth which nourished them. Flame against snow, heat against cold.

The whole affair was like having a terrible mistress who punished you until you fell to your knees, then, laughing cynically, she turned her face and spat dryly on the floor. The French would understand that. The whole world was their double bed.

He turned his perfect profile to the sky from where the shells rained. His eyes were as blue as the sky beyond the snowclouds which covered the fields of praise. He was spotless, inside and out, like a Prussian god who had accidentally descended upon the battlefield to comfort all mankind, to spread his aura of protection over the weak, the frightened and the sordid.

Crunch. Crunch. Stiff leather on crisp snow. Creak Creak. Polished leather encasing his calves.

"What the hell's that?" said Captain Herman Kraft. His unshaven face and bloodshot eyes rising slowly from the depths of the trench and his disembodied head glowering around the countryside searching for the source of the bizarre sound.

"What the hell?" He repeated. "Sound like the Kaiser's guard on parade. No one fucks about out there unless . . ." he broke off as a wounded soldier next to him started coughing convulsively.

"Shhh! . . . Shhh! . . . Quiet. It's bad enough with the shells without having you compete."

The soldier bent double, stuffing his grimy hand against his mouth. Blood seeped through his fingers as he twitched.

Captain Kraft glanced up as a shadow fell across the trench. On a level with his nose was a pair of spotless, shiny boots. German boots. He frowned.

Lieutenant Paul von Przygodsky balanced on the sodden grey sandbags, his grey uniform immaculate, and looked down his nose at the squalor beneath his feet. The stench was disgusting, like foxes and latrines and putrifying flesh.

"I say, is this trench 17A154?"

Captain Kraft blinked. He looked helplessly in both directions along the trench. Was it indeed trench 17A154? He had no idea.

"Ah, yes . . ." he said.

Paul smiled slightly, distantly, like Apollo bestowing half a favour. He clicked his heels, a remarkable feat balanced as he was on the tottering sandbags.

"Lieutenant von Przygodski, reporting for duty, Sir!"

Captain Kraft looked astounded. They looked at each other, the god and the grimy mortal.

Another shell whizzed over their heads and the brilliant flower bloomed in the snow, spraying them with stones and earth. Paul didn't move. He was waiting for the Captain to say something.

"Christ Almighty," thought the Captain, "The man's a complete loony." He glanced sideways at his corporal, who was gawping up at Paul.

"Go and put the soup on, Schultz," Captain Kraft said irrelevantly. To Paul he said, "Would you like to come down here?"

Another shell flew over the trenches in the opposite direction.

"Is it absolutely necessary?" Paul asked with distaste.

"It's customary – yes."

The retaliatory shell screamed back and exploded almost directly behind Paul. The Captain closed his eyes and ducked, expecting blood and bones to spatter him. The blast threw Paul forward and despite himself he found himself in the trench beside Kraft.

Captain Kraft laughed vulgarly. Paul, who had landed neatly on his feet brushed his uniform, a slight crease between his eyes showing his disatisfaction with this turn of events. Stretcher bearers in red-cross arm bands scuttled by carrying their bloody burdens.

"Welcome to the Front, Lieutenant," the Captain said through the smoke. He watched Paul for a moment as he took his handkerchief and flicked it over his boots. "Hm. Yes . . . very smart, I'm sure. New boots."

He turned and led the way to the wooden dug-out. The rough-barked pine logs were covered with a deep layer of snow, and the green branches, which had not been lopped off, looked like miniature Christmas trees. A surreal Christmas, with a background of limbless horses, barbed wire and trees in a blue haze in the distance.

Paul was about to step into the dugout when he saw that it was more disgusting, if that were possible, than the trench. The Captain watched him, an amused smile on his face. He wiped his unwashed hand over his unshaved jaw.

"Well, and what *do* you expect to find here, Lieutenant?"

Paul looked at him as if the question were superfluous. Perfectly seriously he said, rejecting the tin of soup thrust at him by the corporal, "Fame and glory of course – that's what I'm expecting! I'm a Prussian. Military background. My father's a colonel. Heroism is my destiny."

The Captain dipped his face down to his soup tin and looked over the top of it at Paul. He didn't trust himself to speak for a moment. "Is it? Very good."

He drank the soup again, tentatively. "Oh, God, you should be shot, Schultz. If you want heroism you should try Schultz's soup."

Paul glanced up at the sky as if to gain inspiration. His smooth blond head in its neat helmet was profiled against the clean snow like a cut-out on a child's Christmas card and the snow itself looked like the feathery and fern frost patterns on the windows of childhood. The Captain lifted his head, listening. He put the tin down.

"Follow me."

They moved along the trench in single file; above them was an iron fence used as a barricade. The metal work had a lovely shape, snow crystals magnified in black. They were close to the opposite trenches.

The Captain turned, his face a mask of hate. "You can almost smell the enemy's breath, can't you, Lieutenant?"

"Yes, Sir," Paul said automatically, but he wasn't listening. Like a neat dog's, his head was raised as if pointing. In the distance, growing closer, was the sound of cheering. The sound rolled along the trench like the dust and smoke that had earlier filled it.

The Captain continued with his train of thought. "War is one of the most fascinating aspects of human nature. Did you know that?"

A soldier in a bloody grey uniform ran down the trench past them, a foolish grin on his face. "War is over, war is over, war is over." His voice faded as he turned a corner. The Captain ignored him and stared thoughtfully out at the jumble of barren earth and shattered stumps before him. Snow began to fall lightly.

"I say, Sir," Paul said. "The men, Sir, they seem to be cheering. Is that usual?"

"Of course. It's enthusiasm. It's enthusiasm for battle."

Another soldier ran down the trench; he too was grinning foolishly. "The war is over. Peace is declared!" he panted as he ran by.

The Captain also ignored him. "Do you still want fame and honour, Lieutenant?" he said conversationally.

"Yes sir." Paul looked at the soldier's retreating back, then at the Captain's impassive face. "But that chap, Sir . . . he said something about . . ."

The Captain turned his head and looked directly at Paul.

"It's a trick," he said, flatly. "They'll do anything to distract us from our cause. The war will never be over while we're losing."

A group of soldiers ran along the trench, their shoulders forward, pounding like front row forwards, cheering as they ran. "The war is over, Captain . . . Captain . . ."

The Captain waved them over the top of the trench.

"Attack! Attack! Attack!"

"But Captain, the war is over!"

"Attack! Attack! Attack!"

The soldiers started laughing at him, wide grins splitting their mud-splattered thick-stubbled faces. The Captain nodded at Paul and started climbing out of the trench. Paul looked at the men, then shrugged. He followed Captain Kraft and the two of them, lone figures in a white and black landscape, trudged towards the French lines. They were surrounded by cheering, the lost sound rising from the bowels of a hundred trenches, hidden troglodytes performing their secret victory dances. Paul felt himself warming to the sound, felt himself lifted up and carried along on a wave of pride. The benevolent Fatherland would reward all the heroic sons when they returned, victorious. Victorious? He hesitated and paused in mid step. Victorious? The war was over – but who had won?

The blast from the final shell hit him and threw him forward and he knew that the Gods were calling him home at last. The white clouds surrounded him and lifted him up and up, silver light flooding all round as he neared the end of his journey. Any moment now, the music would start.

* * * * *

TWO

Sound the trumpets; beat the drums. Drinking is the Soldiers Pleasure . . . Oh, God, he was thirsty.

What was the nectar of the Gods, apart from nectar? Good German beer, with luck. Cool, golden, sparkling, made with water from a crystal Rhine stream.

Sweet the Pleasure; sweet the Pleasure after Pain. God, he was thirsty and oh, God, how his head hurt. He slowly opened his eyes to the great glowing light, then closed them again quickly. He wasn't ready yet to face the immortals.

"Il se reveille! Il se reveille! Monsieur le Maire, il se reveille!"

The cymbals; the flutes; the trumpets. They were beating him into heaven. If he asked them politely would they reduce the noise before the walls of his inner citadel came tumbling down . . .

It was odd, though, that they were playing La Marseillaise. That was all wrong.

He started to hum the German National Hymn.

Paul opened his eyes cautiously and a sea of curiously-shaped beaming faces pressed down on him, surrounding him on all sides. There was a band, in uniform, and there were children, in ribbons and bonnets, and there were their plump mothers, and there – there was the Mayor. He was conducting the unlikely sextet, waving his arms vigorously, and turning to watch Paul admiringly. Paul glanced up. Ribbons and streamers hung from lamp to lamp and from lamps to floor. Children were tangling themselves and the lamps were swaying as if struck by a wind. Flowers; flowers in vases, and flowers in victorious wreaths, and flowers by the armload. The band played faster. Their uniforms were tattered, but not military in style. The Mayor was draped in sashes and ribbons and bonhomie. He grinned energetically and with one hand, while the other still conducted erratically, he pointed at a huge silk banner which dangled before Paul.

VIVE NOTRE HERO!

The Mayor caught Paul's astonished gaze and smirked proudly. He pointed to the banner again and nodded.

VIVE NOTRE HERO!

So – he had died a hero. But to die a *French* hero . . . What would his father, the Colonel, say?

"What's happened?" he asked in German. "I seem to have lost my memory."

A good-looking girl leaned over Paul and watched his mouth shape the words. She frowned slightly at the Mayor and smiled ravishingly at Paul.

"Çomment?"

"I said, what's happened? Where am I?"

The girl waved at the Mayor, and the Mayor waved at the band. The music died to a creaking halt. Paul focussed on the French helmet dangling from the rail at the foot of his bed. The girl was too close. She looked as if she had one huge eye in the middle of her forehead, but apart from that she wasn't bad at all.

"Çomment?"

The Mayor waddled over to the bed, and he and the girl leaned forward, like vultures.

"Voulez-vous dire quelques chose? Dit!"

Paul's attention was wandering. "Vo ist das Tote Meer?" No that wasn't right. He didn't want the Dead Sea. He wanted to know if he were dead.

"Çomment?" said the girl, stunned.

"Il parle Allemand!" the Mayor wheezed. "Il parle Allemand!"

Everyone pressed closer to look at the horror in the pristine, white bed.

"Non!"

"Oui! Oui! Oui!! Il parle Allemand."

"C'est un Allemand!"

"Un Boche!"

The Mayor grabbed Paul by the collar of his crisp pyjamas and attempted to drag him upright, then released him so that his head crashed back against the pillows.

The Mayor suddenly was aware of all the heroic trappings adorning the room. He started to tear down the ribbons, threw the flowers at the open door, and at the same time he shooed the children before him like chickens in a farmyard, and ushered the band and their bulky instruments out of the room.

There was a collision in the door, while the Mayor continued to hurl the flowers and scream in broken German-accented English: "We thought you were one of us ... we thought you were our hero ... you fiend, to deceive us ... you Boche ..."

He turned rapidly and yanked the pillow from under Paul's bandaged head and Paul felt his wound re-open. Blood seeped into the sheets. The Mayor started to grab at the blankets, and the girl, seeing his intention, tried to prevent him.

"No, no, he is sick. He is injured."

"Ha! Sick is he! You've lain there, lying to us ... eating our bread ... drinking our wine ... sleeping in our bed ... with our pillows ... eyeing our girls ..."

"But he's been in a coma – he's eaten nothing —"

"Deceiving us ... arriving here, naked ... wearing only the helmet of our Motherland. Mon Dieu!"

"But he's had a coma!"

"Coma! Coma! Comaaagh!" He spat. "Je m'en fous se son coma!"

The room was empty; faces peered round the corner of the door and there were screams in the corridor beyond. The Mayor pushed the girl out with his fat belly as he dragged at the remnants of the flowers. He remembered, when he got to the door, and turned, to yank the French helmet from the end of the bed and then the door was slammed shut, and Paul was left lying alone in a raped room, his bleeding head dangling over the edge of the bed, the blankets half way across the floor.

"But if I'm not their hero, who am I?" he said aloud. His memory had completely gone, the final bang had completed what the shell had started.

Sweet the Pleasure after Pain. The pleasure had yet to come and heaven would have to wait for its misplaced hero.

* * * * *

THREE

It was odd, what the fisherman had said. "A lot of things used to be Germany."

Paul frowned as he shuffled along through the springing grass of a new season. The vivid growth, the damp weeds, were covering the tortured land. He had been away a long time, then. But why wouldn't someone tell him what was happening?

This used to be Germany the fisherman said. "Ja, ja – Deutschland." But now, it was his property and he was French – Salut.

When he found his regiment again, all would be clear. Captain What's 'is name, though, he wouldn't be there. Paul had a very clear image of the Captain – who the hell was he? – cartwheeling through the air, outlined against the piled, white clouds. That was the one lasting and pure image in his whole head. Just Captain What's 'is name flying through the sky. Nothing before and nothing after.

Paul climbed up a steep bank through an entanglement of budding beeches. The leaves were not yet broken through the beetle-brown cases, but the land underfoot was covered with soft woodland grass. He wanted to nestle his face in it and try to bring his memory back by making his aching head cool. The blood pounded, round and round all the time, with the constant effort of trying to remember. If only he could remember what it was that he *didn't* remember, then he would soon remember all that he had forgotten. That didn't make much sense to him either, but, then, nothing much did.

"A lot of things used to be Germany – Salut!" That was clear enough in principle – but what the hell did it mean in fact?

Iron tracks, iron sheds, iron trains. It was a dead grey and white world but it would lead him to life and to memory and to Berlin.

Paul stumbled along the tracks, ignoring the possibility of a train mowing him down. There was a man with a pick axe, working by the side of the tracks, and beyond him the long line of a stationary freight train, stretching into the distance.

It was so long that the end could not see its beginning.

"I have a problem," Paul said with no preamble, as if he were already introduced and half-way through a conversation.

The worker jumped. "A problem?"

"I must get back to Berlin before the end of the war ..." Paul clutched his arm.

The worker smiled slightly and nodded. "You're right ... you have a problem." He turned. Paul caught him again by his arm.

"What do you mean?"

"The war ended – over a year ago ..."

Paul stared at him disconcerted. "My God," he thought. "I've lost my memory and now I've lost my mind. I'm going mad."

The worker nodded at the freight train, which was slowly moving in a series of disjointed shunts. "If you want to go to Berlin, that train's your best bet."

Paul continued to stare at him. The word Berlin suddenly penetrated the fog he felt he was swimming through; a fog of porridge. His head ached with a sharper rush of blood. Then he turned and stumbled towards the train and leapt into a half-closed car. The train was picking up speed. Paul stuck his head through the door. He was on his knees.

"Who won?" he screamed into the wind.

"Nobody."

Paul fell back into a corner of the car and looked up at the head of a tethered horse. The horse stopped chewing some hay and stared unblinkingly at Paul.

"Nobody? Nobody? That's impossible."

He drew his knees up to his chin and continued to address the horse. "Somebody always wins."

He stared around the dark interior of the car, which was full of animals, of which the horse was the only one tethered.

"My God," he said, "We lost the war ..."

A small pink pig, very clean, wandered over to Paul and rooted about in his clothes. Paul listlessly let him do it, and the pig eventually gave up his search for food and snuggled down next to Paul with contended groans, snuffles and snorts. Paul put his arm over the pig, and cuddled together they fell asleep as the train rocked on to Berlin.

He had been walking for hours it seemed, and the pig was heavy in his arms. He could feel its plump warmth through his dark blue wool coat.

Spring had not yet reached Berlin and the city was uncompromisingly cold and bleak. Gaunt buildings, like aging hacks, cobbled streets, shiny with a recent fall of rain that would soon turn to snow. Trams rattled over the cobbles, filled with workers in blue denim and black peaked caps. Trotting carriages filled with women, furs and feathers. Rich bitches, but with dead faces. Only the children sparkled as they ran with their hoops. Children never gave in, not even during the bad times. Like a seed growing under rocks, they found their way to the top, vigorous and springing.

Paul stopped to look at the mighty Victory arch with its high-stepping horses.

"Look, pig," he said. "We won, once."

The pig grunted in ecstasy. The end of Paul's long woollen scarf was hanging tantalisingly close to the pig's neat little snout, and he eyed it with interest. Paul had given the pig all the food he had been able to forage, saving none for himself on the principle that a pig's hunger was stronger than his own. But, even so, Paul was hungry. One needed money to eat. If he could discover his family it would help; they would feed him.

The important thing was to remember who, and where, they were.

He raised his head and listened to some strange, contorted music which expressed all he felt. He would follow it to its source like a child following the Pied Piper.

As Paul walked he noticed that he was walking parallel with a depressed queue of depressed people. At the head of the queue, and guarded by barbed wire, was a huge steaming iron cauldron of soup and each person was ladled out a helping before the next shuffled into place. The soup looked thin and watery, made perhaps of leeks, or potatoes.

"'Bout time they put in a couple of ham bones or a couple of slices of bacon," one woman muttered to her neighbour. "Ain't seen meat for months."

Paul pulled the pig closer to his body and slunk by the queue to the corner of the Chamisso Plaz Master where a small group of drab whores chatted near the Litvas Sâule, their faces devoid of any animation, only the sweeping display of feathers in their outrageous hats lending some colour to the scene.

Paul began to feel faint again. Hunger griped his stomach but it was more his efforts to remember things that made him palpitate with terror at the mist which seemed to dog him. Things looked very small and far away, as if seen through the thick bottom of a used glass. As he looked, they got smaller and smaller, receding from him until he felt like a huge, floating diver with lead in his feet and gas in his head.

Sounds grew fainter and he was very tired. He and the pig should soon have to lie down, snuggled close to absorb warmth and friendship before his body stretched into two distinct parts and his lower regions sank into the mire, while his head and heart floated off into space.

He knew that he wasn't destined for Olympus any longer, although at some point he had been. The icy, sharp brightness of the far reaches of space called him like a distant threnody. He had forgotten about the singing that had drawn him there in the first place, and it was the ungainly horse which drew his focus back into the square. The horse pranced about like a demented caricature of the one he had shared a car with on the train to Berlin. It moved and grimaced and reared and wobbled its rear quarters and he thought it was all part of his illusions and the dream-like quality in which everything was painted.

It was when he started to read the horse's coat that he realised it was made of papier mache and canvas, and the outside layer was plastered with sheets of newspaper on which all the news was left wing. The next thing he realised was that it was dancing grotesquely to the music.

Clop, squirm, prance, preen; with each convulsion the girl on the makeshift platform screamed her revolutionary tirade at the pre-occupied crowd who had nothing better to do, since they had no food to fill their aching bellies, but to listen.

"All of you . . . stop whatever you're doing before it's too late . . ."

Too late for what? Paul thcught as he looked at her dumbly.

She was dressed, as were most of the people he had seen, in blue denim with a peaked cap on which there was a red badge. Her scarf was red and her lovely vital face, framed by a tumble of yellow curls. She was the most vibrant thing about the day, about the city and about the journey to find his home. She was also endearingly familiar, but he thought he could have dreamed about someone like her.

"Aren't you all tired of being oppressed, bludgeoned, harrassed, tyrannized, tortured, sucked, grounded, flattened?" The crowd and Paul edged closer. He knew that he had seen her before and the excitement started to stir, clearing the fog a little, not like a knife, cleanly, but like a feather duster, a little flicker here and a little flicker there.

"Living in rat-ridden remnants of ... of ..." she paused and looked helplessly behind her at the horse to prompt her.

It was the childish gesture, the downcurl of her mouth and the movements of her hands which reminded Paul of his childhood playmate.

"Cilly!"

"What's that word again?" Cilly asked the horse, while Paul stared at her in shy delight.

"Despondence," said the horse's ass.

"... despondence! Eating peanuts on toilets while the real elephants are sipping absinthe, dining in decent rooms ..."

The crowd pressed closer and Cilly, loving the attention of the people grew more theatrical in her gestures. She flung her arms and her chest out, "Are we warriors or woodworms?"

She jumped from the cart and grabbed at the tattered lapels of the nearest man and screamed into his face, "Are we going around in tatters of yesteryear?"

Her hand jerked down and the lapel ripped and hung down. The owner of the torn jacket frowned and looked down at his coat. Before he could protest, Cilly was running her hand over his rough face with careless familiarity, "... with unshaven faces ..." and on over his greasy hair ... "... wax in our ears ..."

The man backed away, his furious face showing that he was insulted, but Cilly ignored him, turning her back to the crowd, screaming, "No!!! We've got to raise ourselves to new heights."

She ran and jumped back again onto the cart and started singing the revolutionary song with great energy that had drawn Paul to her in the first place, but the crowd no longer was with her. They were pressing in on Paul, their attention focused with great salivating intensity on the pig.

Paul suddenly looked up and the grotesque faces were all around him; narrow foreheads, long noses, bulging eyes, wide, enormously wide, cheekbones and great red dripping tongues. Contorted faces, faces like the ones he had seen in the hospital in France. Their tongues moved slowly over their bloated lips and his pig was so many sausages vanishing down their gaping throats.

Paul clutched the pig and began to run while the starving crowd streamed after him. He could hear their dedicated breath, their determined feet pounding over the cobbles and the pig grunted in soft ecstasy.

"Come back, come back!" screamed Cilly.

"You don't understand, you don't understand," sobbed Paul.

"This is all I have brought back from the war . . . just a pig . . ."

Cilly yelled at the fleeing crowd, "How do you expect to win a revolution if all you're interested in is food?"

But there was no-one left who cared. Already the pig was sausages and black pudding and larded hams and chitterlings and jellied trotters and chewy cheeks and chops with kidneys and pate dressed with red peppers. The little pig was feeding the five thousand and five thousand lips drooled in anticipation.

Paul ran over some grass and ducked into a heavy wrought iron doorway. He leaned against the wall behind the door, gasping, his heart pounding against the pig who was making soft snorts of delight, not the harsh grunts from a pig-pen, but the gentle snuffling sounds made by puppies feeding. Outside, the crowd streamed by, then stopped and walked aimlessly about, knowing that they had lost the pig but not certain what to do next.

Paul looked down the corridor of the apartment block

where he was and saw a list of names on the wall.

Pension von Przygodski. 2 Stock.

He read it through slowly, then read it again. It still said the same.

Pension von Przygodski. 2 Stock.

The name was remarkably familiar; so familiar that it must have some connection with him. His hand reached out automatically to press the light switch, and he paused, looking at his hand and the switch. That hand had known where to find that switch. Ergo; the switch was also familiar. He was – he must be on home ground.

There was a wild baying from the stairs and he pressed back against the wall and the pig wallowed feebly at this new threat.

"Sit ... sit ... sit ..." came a melodious but desperate voice, and a beautiful woman came flying down the stairs like Diana dragged by her two huge hounds.

The great black and white beasts flew at Paul and he cowered back. The pig was split in two and vanishing down their throats, its little pink tail twirling like a frantic windmill while somewhere deep inside one of the dogs – he wasn't sure which one it was – came the stifled grunts from its dear little snout. Paul turned his back to the dogs, while the woman, dressed in the most fashionable clothes in Berlin, clung gamely to the leads.

"I beg your pardon," she said in well-bred accent as she whizzed by Paul, her coat swirling and her feathers flying.

Her eyes suddenly widened as she noted his blond beauty, but the hounds had borne her off into the air where Diana hunted and Circe reigned. The pig heaved a sigh and collapsed back into Paul's arms, safe again.

It was his home, of course. He was the son of the house, home from the War, crowned not with laurels but bearing a pig. He looked about him.

Nothing looked the same. It looked so . . . so crowded . . . so vulgar. Yes, that was it. It was vulgar.

"Mutti?" he called and waited. Silence.

"Mutti!"

He walked down the corridor and glanced in at the first

room, where the door was wide open.

"Mutti?" he said before he realised that after three years this could not be his mother.

The enormous tart stared back at him, her emerald green dress using so many yards of material that it would have curtained the salon windows. Red feathers wound their way over her vast bosom and bellies. Tall red feathers waved in her hair. Her painted face showed anger and her small eyes glittered. She was the queen pig in her farmyard of a littered room. Fans, feathers, petticoats, stays, stockings. The heavy scent of sex and dust. "Off with his head! Off with his head!"

The heavy axe swung, and Paul backed away and moved on looking for his mother.

It was his home – and this was his room. The china doll on his bed stared back at him. Her face was white and her cheeks painted a round of pink, the line between the colours perfectly distinct. She was like a Japanese doll. Satin draped her slender body and shiny silk stockings her legs. He could see the shadow at the top of her thighs where the welt of the stockings merged into the smooth cream of her flesh. The sight unmoved him. A black satin band and a rose were fastened round her slender throat and her eyes were black-lashed and sultry.

Paul looked at the man who was lying next to her on the bed.

The man stared back. The room was such a mess with feminine underwear and intimate articles that the painted doll belonged, but the man did not.

"What are you doing in my room?" Paul addressed the man.

The woman answered. "In your room, darling?" She lifted her brows and grinned mockingly, provocatively. "... This is my room darling."

"No, no, this is my room." Paul looked around distracted. "This is my room. I remember perfectly clearly now. This *is* my room. I don't know what's happening here, but this is definitely my room ...

"I might have lost the Kaiser ... I might have lost the regiment ... I might even have lost the war "

The woman started laughing. Paul grew angrier.

"... But if you think that I'm going to lose this room ..."

She nodded, a cynical smile flitting across the china mask.

"... well, you're crazy ..." Paul concluded.

The woman opened her legs languidly and turned to the man suggestively. Paul backed away again and looked hopelessly along the corridor.

"Mutti!"

The pig looked up at him with interest and Paul heaved it up. He had been carrying it for days it seemed, and it was getting heavier all the time.

A voice came from above him. "All the rooms are taken."

There was a pause as Paul stopped. The voice continued musingly.

"But I think we could find room for your pig."

Paul glanced up. The woman, and owner of the voice, was peering at him out of the bathroom fanlight ... Her hair was tangled sliding from the many pins which stuck out at crazy angles, and behind her he could make out a washing line near the ceiling full of black lace petticoats all dripping into the bath below.

"Aunt Hilda!"

The woman stared. There was a sudden crash as she fell from view and after several moments scrambling, the bathroom door flew open.

"Paul! ... Oh my God! ... We thought you were dead!"

"No, I'm not dead. I'm very much alive."

"Yes ... yes ..." Hilda said, distracted.

She came forward and peered at Paul. She was plumper than he remembered and wore a black and yellow satin shirt striped like a wasp.

"But ... but ... How long have you been alive?"

"Ever since I can remember." He thrust the pig at her which she took with a startled look of anticipation and pleasure.

"Look," Paul said, "What is going on here?"

Hilda looked at the pig with growing interest, and spoke to herself. "Paul's back. Paul's back. Ohhhh – what a mess."

"Yes, it was a mess. Explosions usually are."

Hilda glanced directly at Paul. "You know, your mother's going to faint if she sees you ..."

"Ah yes. Where is Mutti?"

"She can explain it better than I can," Hilda said desperately, jerking her chin to encompass the whole chaotic flat. "She's at the Turkish bath."

Paul looked stunned. "What on earth is she doing there?"

Hilda hesitated then wet her lips. She glanced doubtfully at Paul. "An activity she took up at the end of the war . . . it's called work."

"Working? My mother working!"

Paul turned on his heel and marched, military style down the passage towards the front door while Hilda looked despairingly at his retreating back and with interest at the pig.

"Paul, come back!"

"I want those people out of my room, Aunt Hilda," Paul shouted just before he slammed the door. "I want them out before I get back."

* * * * *

FOUR

"Oh yes," said Mutti as she poured the champagne, "They wanted to award him the Iron Cross, y'know, but I told them not to bother – but to keep their metal for the war effort."

She smiled brightly through the steam at the voluptuous naked bodies draped on marble steps and marble slabs around a gently bubbling central pool.

"At the end, all he had to defend himself was a handful of rocks . . ."

Greta, another masseuse raised her eyes to heaven as she pounded at her particular mound of dimpled, quivering flesh.

"Oh God," she confided, "There she goes again. She never stops talking about her son."

". . . But his love for his Fatherland gave him the courage he needed, and while the bombs were whizzing over his head . . ."

"Pass me another grape, darling."

"Syphilis, did you say?"

"And lots and lots of gonorrhoea."

. . . and the enemy tanks were moving towards him, he saluted the bodies of his dead comrades and committed suicide! My poor son." Mutti stood up straight, a bottle of champagne in one hand and saluted with the other. Her hand continued over her short blonde hair and white scarf as she wiped the sweat from her face. She paused, staring through the enveloping clouds of steam.

"Oh my God," she said, "The hallucinations are coming back."

"What hallucinations?" Greta asked derisively.

"Of my poor Paul," Mutti said faintly. "I often see his face in front of me with his sensitive, bewildered expression." Greta grinned maliciously and suggestively, while Mutti continued to stare through the steam.

"Where the hell is my mother working?" Paul thought as he stared at her and at the silver bowls crammed with fruits, the magnums of champagne, and the servants spraying the bodies of the rich with fresh water and perfumed salts as if they were tending gross tropical orchids in a greenhouse. He hadn't heard what she had been saying because of the gramophone which was horning out an American jazz tune.

"Paul?" Mutti said incredulously as the vision refused to go away. She moved towards him cautiously and delicately extended her hand. Trembling, she ran a finger down his cheek, and when she felt his flesh, she snatched back her hand with a gasp.

"The War Department lied to me!"

"War Department?" Paul repeated inanely.

"They said you were dead!"

"I'm not."

"I see that. But I had to believe someone." Mutti looked about her furtively to catch the reaction of the others in the baths.

"He's been gone some time, you know," she said defensively.

"I had a lot of difficulties," Paul said diffidently. "Hospitals, that kind of thing."

Mutti started to shake, but whether with anger or with shock she could not tell.

"Oh my God, you've been dead for months! And now you just walk in as if you're alive! You could have chosen a better way to *resurrect*." She emphasised the last word, glancing sideways at Greta, as if that would explain everything, lending her son's sudden reappearance the aura of a miracle.

"I brought you a pig," Paul said vaguely.

His mother stared at him as if he were mad. "A pig?"

Paul was silent. He had a feeling he had said the wrong thing. Mutti rallied. "My boy, if your father knows that all you brought back from the war was a *pig* – why, he'll have another paralysis."

"Another what?"

So this was the hero he had always wanted to emulate. He sat in a wheel chair, padded and upholstered like a tapestry throne his hands urgently clutching the armrests and gazing fixedly into a space where no dreams existed.

Paul looked about him, at the crowded tables littered with photographs of military parades, officer groups, the Kaiser, and of his father, the Colonel, in his days of glory. Photographs were all he would ever be now.

"How long?" Paul asked.

"Since the end of the war," Mutti said with pride. "Since they proclaimed the Republic."

"Yes, yes," Hilda said, pressing in eagerly. "The blow was oo much for him . . ."

They stared at him fondly, the man who refused to acknowledge anything that existed today.

"He chose that particular chair. We fixed it up nicely for him, you can see," Mutti said. "It's a shame he won't recognise you."

Paul waved his hand before the old man's face, but the faded blue eyes didn't even blink.

"Vati! Vati!" Mutti said urgently.

"It's no good," said Hilda.

"Vati, what day is it today?" Mutti tried. She turned to Paul. "You see, nothing. Actually, I think he's just pretending. He won't admit defeat."

Paul recognised the unbending pride and logic in his father's actions, and he clicked his heels and saluted. "Father, we may have been defeated, but we haven't lost the war. Sold-out politicians stabbed us in the back!"

His mother nudged him and edged him out of the throne-room.

"Ssh," she said very loudly, turning to look at her husband, "Don't excite him – he gets jittery."

The Colonel sat as if he were carved of stone and Paul wondered how his jitteriness manifested itself.

They moved into the living-room and were followed by an elegant man in his forties, who apparently had materialised from one of the bedrooms. He had the bearing of a cavalry officer in mufti, but Paul had the feeling there was something odd about him. He realised after a moment that one of these truancies was the fact that he gave himself away by his inept handling of his monocle.

Hilda suddenly darted out of the living-room and reappeared wheeling the Colonel. She pushed his chair up close to one of the tall windows. The Colonel would have been able to see the view if the lace curtains had been pulled back, but it did not occur to Hilda to do this. She smiled fondly at the back of the old man's head, well satisfied by her thoughtfulness.

Paul thought vaguely that he would take his father for walks, and things – show him the town, talk to him, show him that he admired his honourable gesture to the Kaiser.

He looked meaningly at the stranger, waiting for an introduction, but his mother was flapping around, pulling at the stranger's clothes.

"Let me look at you . . ."

"Wilhelmina, we'll be late," the stranger said, irritated at being fussed over before the beautiful young man who was looking at him so cynically. He raised his eyebrows towards Paul and the monocle fell out. "Wilhelmina?" he said, leaving the question hanging in the air.

Mutti collected herself. "Oh, Major . . . this is my son, Paul," she said almost casually. Already she had accepted the miracle of Paul's return from the grave.

"I don't think I understand," the Major frowned. "Your son? . . ." "Oh yes," Hilda said vaguely. "He was dead, but now he's not . . . dead, I mean."

"Oh, I see," the Major said, not seeing at all. The boy was remarkably handsome, and if he were the son, things would have to be tackled diplomatically. It was one thing with the Colonel *non compos mentis*, but it was another matter with this beautiful boy at the head of the household. He could see he might have to tread carefully. These damned Prussians were so bloody touchy.

He clicked his heels. "Major Alexander von Mueller," he said, making an effort to be polite.

Paul returned the bow distantly.

"You look fit enough," the Major said. "What was the story – some girl, eh?" he winked and the monocle fell out again.

Paul stared back at him perplexed, while his mother turned to him with a little cry of reproach.

"Paul, how could you!"

"But, Mutti, I was in hospital – in *France* . . . I had lost my memory."

The Major grinned ferociously. "A nurse! It's always a

French nurse!"

Paul glared at him. "Don't be so ridiculous." He decided to attack his mother. It was obvious that the bogus Major was her responsibility.

"Mutti, why have you let my room?"

"But we had to," Mutti said in an anxious rush. "We simply had to – but I assure you that yours was the last – the very last! – to go ... the situation was desperate, and the Major here came to our assistance ..."

"I bet he did," Paul thought cynically.

"... changing the place into a guesthouse ... why, me working at the Turkish bath was his idea ..."

Paul curled his lip.

"... and I don't know what I would have done without him," she concluded feebly, her misty blue eyes swimming.

"Last year the Spartakists had their machine gun nest here," Hilda added. "We spent a whole week in the cellar. Your mother was bitten by a rat."

"Yes!" Mutti affirmed, pulling up her skirt. Paul averted his eyes.

"They used the bathroom – everything ..." Hilda said. "The Collected Works of Goethe ... everything."

"Oh, there was a paper shortage as well, was there?" Paul said rudely.

"Major, he brought us a pig," Mutti said hurriedly.

"A pig? Well, that's wonderful," the Major's eyes suddenly gleamed. He licked his lips.

Paul turned to his aunt. He had forgotten his dear little pig.

"Yes, where is my pig?"

Hilda tried to look vague, her face a mask of guilt. She patted her pockets absentmindedly, looking around the room as she backed towards the door. "Pig . " she said brightly. Everyone glared at her. "Hilda! The pig!"

"Oh, the pig ... it's somewhere ... somewhere ... now, *where* did I ...?" she fished in her pockets again, then she was at the door and through it. Her voice was heard from the passage ... "Pig ... now where *did* I ...?"

He was dreaming again of the last day in the trenches. The

memories had evaded him for over a year, and now they were returning with a painful and disjointed frequency at night. It was as if the hail of fire had divided not his life, but himself in two.

In the life before he had all the price of Prussia in his blood; after, he was an empty shell who gestured and postured but it meant nothing. He was an internal cripple and that was worse than being a visual cripple with no limbs. How could he explain that he felt as if he had become his own abortion – that his inner man had evacuated through his bowels along with all the shit and all the blood that had once flowed through him, sustaining the officer and the gentleman he had been bred to be?

"Fire, fire, attack . . ."

"You can almost smell their breath," the Captain had said.

"Attack! Attack!"

Paul woke with a start and sat bolt upright on his narrow cot. He was in a box room, emptied of everything but the barest essentials, his own room lost to him forever he thought. Even if the whores left he wouldn't want to return to it; this barren cell suited him.

A snowball hit the window, splatting like frosted soufflé. Lots of balls had been thrown and it was their hollow bang bang that had awoken him. Paul peered through the circles of snow and saw Cilly on an upper balcony across the well. She was standing in the snow on the wrought-iron work dressed in a pink satin robe, a pink feather boa draped about her neck. She was laughing and looked very beautiful. Paul lifted one arm in a weak wave and Cilly waved back energetically.

"Paul, it's me. I'm coming down."

She waved gaily and disappeared with a flick of the boa and a swirl of pink satin.

Paul lay back and put his arms under his head. From where he lay he could see the sky. It was grey and heavy with snow. It was like the battlefield sky on the last day. Somewhere beyond, it was brilliant, heavenly blue. Somewhere below, under the snow, were the secret colours of the crocus and iris and daffodils. He liked bright, sharp yellow.

It suggested bravery and courage. It was the colour of the sun. He hadn't seen the sun for a long, long time.

Cilly poked at the egg yolk with a delicate finger, and Hilda slapped her hand.

"Is this Paul's breakfast?" Cilly asked.

"It is," Hilda said huffily as she arranged a careful tray and stood back to admire the effect. She glanced at Cilly. The girl looked outrageous, like a nightclub tart on honeymoon.

"Well, Cilly, to what do we owe the unexpected visit of our housekeeper's socialist daughter?"

Cilly laughed and scooped up the tray. "I'll take it," she said ignoring the question.

Hilda gazed after the swinging door. "She didn't even say hello . . . these lower classes have no charm!"

"Hello, Cilly," Paul said frowning at her. He was sitting up in bed, his arms crossed protectively over his chest and a definite black cloud lowered over his brow.

Cilly grinned. She tried to look sexy, but she was so pleased to see Paul that the grin broke through again.

"Morning, war hero. Remember me . . .?" she lifted the hem of her robe with one hand, the tray balanced precariously in the other. Paul seemed shocked. "Remember me . . . Identification mark: scar, left thigh, Wintergarten skating lesson, clumsy cadet. Remember?"

She moved across to the bed and sat down at the foot, then moved up level with Paul's hips. "So you're really back . . . After three years!"

She put the tray on Paul's chest and began to toy with the hairs she could see above it.

"Grown a hair or two or three or four . . . big boy now!"

"Do you mind?" Paul said huffily.

Cilly was determined to ignore his mood. She tossed her own voluptuous, silky curls, a darker shade of the classic gold of Paul's hair.

"Mine's worn different now. Do you like it?"

"It's okay," Paul said without conviction.

"Well, I've tried a hundred styles," she prattled. "They all look wonderful on me! Just wonderful!"

"I wouldn't know." Coldly. "You never sent me a picture."

"How could I – you never wrote."

They looked at each other and Cilly burst out laughing. She leaned forward and rumpled his hair, while Paul reared back.

"I dreamed of you getting blinded by mustard gas so I could guide you for ever and ever."

"How sweet."

"I thought so too. Well, darling, I'm glad to see you're the same senseless oaf you were before the war."

"The war wasn't quite what I expected," Paul said stiffly. He decided he would punish Cilly, but wasn't sure for what. He wanted her to react in some hurt way. No one seemed to care very much about him now that he was back.

"We all thought you'd died."

"Why does everyone keep maliciously insinuating that I'm dead when I'm not? I'm *alive*! This house is full of sneaky, scheming people who have absolutely no respect for the wounded."

Cilly stood up and moved towards the door. "Poor oaf. Poor wounded oaf," she said lovingly. She paused hand on hip and gave a sexy shrug to her shoulder. "By the way, darling, did you know I'm one of the working classes most popular artists?"

"Well, I know you sing in the streets," Paul said rudely.

"Well, darling, we can't all be war heroes. You should join us – you could play all the military parts."

"Don't be childish, Cilly. I'm an officer."

"Ooh. Pardon me. Silly of me to forget." She whisked out of the door, giving him a quick flash of one perfect calf.

Paul lay back in his bed and contemplated the congealed egg on the plate. His coffee had a skin on it. There was no doubt about it – Cilly was not the sweet young thing she had been before he went away. He wondered idly if she had a lover.

He had been told that there was a job for officers going at a publicity agency. At least it would be better than working in the hell of the Turkish bath at the beck and call of the degenerate rich, who somehow had been able to keep all their money. Hilda had kitted him out with a uniform as well, one that had belonged to her poor dead husband she had said with tears in her eyes. The bullet hole over the breast had been slightly disconcerting, but at least it showed that one member of the family at least had died with a bullet in him. Paul had the feeling that everyone thought that it was he who should have been the dead hero in the family. Now his mother had nothing to talk about to all her friends.

Paul tramped along the cobbles in his ill-fitting uniform. He had tidied himself up, of course. Jobs in publicity were notoriously glamorous, but there wasn't much he could do about the bullet hole. It was unfortunately on the wrong side to pin a medal – even supposing he had any. His father, naturally, had several, but they were all for earlier campaigns and anyone who knew about these things would immediately assume that he was a poseur and not a wounded officer.

Paul glanced down at the hole again. It wasn't too big. He imagined his uncle's life oozing out of that hole. It would, of course, have been more dramatic if there were a parallel hole at the back.

Whizzz! In and Poww! Out!

He was at the address given him by Major von Mueller. Hateful man – Paul resented anything he did for him, resented the job the Major had got him at the Turkish bath, and knew that however glamorous or highly paid, he would resent the publicity job as well.

The address was correct – but the ambiance was all wrong.

The railway arches stretched along the shabby, cobbled street and under the arch, ill-lit with bare bulbs on dangerously long wires, was the run-down warehouse, all iron girders and rust. It looked like an iron mill in Dante's 'Inferno', supposing there had been such a thing. At any rate, it certainly looked a hell of a place to send him. Groups of men strolled about in sandwich boards and bicyclists weaved in and out of a long line of gigantic green-grey bottles which appeared to be chatting to each other.

Paul approached an official-looking man who sat alone at a trestle table in this sea of insanity.

The man glanced up. "Ah. You must be the sixth bottle."

"Major von Mueller sent me," Paul said stiffly.

"I know who sent you! Save your breath. Name?"

"Przygodski."

The man wrote carefully, then rose and led Paul to a bottle lying on the ground. Paul looked numbly into the interior. It was made of plywood and canvas, like Cilly's horse. He frowned at its immense size, not appreciating yet that he was to wear the bottle. Two other bottles started to fool around, doing a little dance, a neat pair of feet peeping out from the base of each one. They playfully clinked necks.

"Come on, come on! Cut it out!" the Supervisor shouted. "Time to line up and get moving." He turned to Paul. "This is your bottle. Keep it clean and tidy, bring it back on Friday. No bottle – no pay."

Paul nodded dumbly. His bottle. He couldn't believe the ignominy of it. It was all Major Mueller's fault! God, how he must be laughing!

"What's your new job, Paul?"

"I'm a bottle, Mutti."

Paul ducked into the bottle, assisted by the Supervisor and a small boy. He swayed alarmingly.

"Come on, bottles line up!" the Supervisor shouted above the sudden roar of a train from the arches. "Come on now, stop pretending you're all champagne. Alexanderplatz, Ku'damm, left side. Right side, Leipzigerstrasse. Come on – hey, sixth bottle pay attention – Potsdamer Platz. Go on, go on, get a move on."

"I can't see. I can't breathe in here," Paul's voice echoed distantly. It was nearly impossible to hear him at all, let alone understand what he was saying.

The Supervisor rose on his toes and peered through Paul's eye-level grille. "Turn your head, you idiot!" He groaned. "Oh God, it's hopeless – I've been sent an idiot here."

Paul fell over, and like some strange tortoise threshed on the cobbles. A sandwich man peered through the grille, then tipped some water through the opening to revive Paul who appeared unconscious.

"Poor baby! He thinks he was the only one to go to war!"

Eventually Paul righted himself with the help of the small

boy, and in single file, the grotesque regiment of bottles walked through the railway arches and into the wide open wastes of Berlin.

* * * * *

FIVE

Paul sighed wearily as he slowly mounted the stairs to the flat. It was difficult navigating the corners in the bottle, but he could hardly carry it up the stairs, and even less, leave it in the street. They had said nothing about how he was supposed to store the bottle at night and it was certainly too wide to pass through the door of the flat.

He left it on the landing outside the flat's front door. There was just enough room to squeeze by, both into the flat and to the floor above. It would have to do he was too tired to care.

The flat smelled of warmth and home cooking. Hilda was in the kitchen, baking cookies.

Paul smiled at her as he reached out a hand for one of the rich biscuits. "You're up late, Aunt Hilda."

"Leave my cookies! It was bad enough getting the butter without having you gobble them up."

"They're good . . . why are you cooking so late?"

"If I don't use the butter up now, it will go in the night. Rats."

"But won't the rats eat the cookies?"

"They won't be able to.' Grimly. "I'm taking the tin to bed with me, but I could hardly tuck butter under my pillow."

Paul grinned faintly. God, he was tired, and hell, he was tired of the houseguests, as his mother insisted on calling them.

"How's your new job, Paul?"

"Okay, I suppose. A bit confining . . ."

His aunt did not ask him what the job was. She nodded vaguely as she carefully lifted the cookies into the tin, counting them as she did so.

"There!" Triumphantly. "Now I know how many there are, if they go in the night, I'll know it!"

"Bit late then," Paul suggested.

"Yes, well, never mind – at least I'll know it."

Paul reached out for another cookie before the tin was closed. Hilda snatched it to her bosom. "Oh, come on do make yourself useful. Take these flowers that have come for Eva. Lovely, eh? Take them to her room but don't forget to put them in a vase!"

She handed Paul an enormous bunch of waxy yellow tulips and he walked slowly to Eva's room. It had once been his father's study, when the flat had been smart. The walls had been lined with bookshelves and heavy oil paintings of the dogs and horses at the house in the country. He had no idea what had happened to the country place. Tomorrow he would ask.

Paul nearly gasped as he gazed round the room that was now Eva's, whoever she was. The room was full to the point of overspilling like some exotic second-hand shop, full of mystery and magic.

Snake's head lanterns curved over and shed pools of light on crowded tables and silken cushions. Paintings of purple and white peacocks, carved screens, stained glass windows on the cabinet doors, feathers in vases and crystal bottles of scent.

Paul dumped the flowers on a divan and looked at the bottles on the cluttered dressing table. His pure profile and smooth cap of golden hair were reflected in the three mirrors. He picked up a bottle and unscrewed the top and sniffed it in a kind of religious fervour. He remembered the smell. His head swam – where had he smelled this before, this cloying yet sharp scent?

He glanced down at a small table next to him and saw the perfect face he had seen on his first day in Berlin. It was Diana of the hounds.

He picked up the photograph and studied it, feeling waves of adoration astonishingly pass through his limbs until he felt faint. What was this effect she had on him, this unknown woman? Was it because he had seen her first when he had found his home and his memory again?

A deep but subdued growling. Paul froze and slowly turned his head. Two great dogs, their eyes gleaming like fiery coals in the light from the snake's head lamps, were glaring at him from behind a screen. They slowly bared their huge fangs and Paul felt his legs turn to jelly. To survive the war and be eaten by dogs!

The dogs stood up and they seemed more huge than he remembered. With one leap they were upon him and he went flying over onto the divan where the tulips were. He grabbed at the bunch and vainly shielded himself with them. The dogs placed their four huge front paws on his chest and breathed tongues of fire down his throat. A playful swipe and half the tulips went flying. Another playful swipe and his skin would be shredded. From his angle Paul did not see their tails wagging; he remembered only the story of the dogs whose eyes were as big as dinner plates. He had no tinderbox, but he was a soldier.

"Castor! Pollux!" said an amused voice. "Stop it at once. Come on, now, sit!"

The dogs loped to their mistress, lolling tongues and smiling mouths showing their pleasure in her return.

"What are you doing on my bed?" she asked Paul, a lift to her brow.

Unaccountably Paul blushed scarlet. He stammered. "I . . . I . . . can explain . . . my aunt . . . the old lady . . . that is . . . the one with the curly hair . . . these flowers . . ." He held out the tattered remnants of the yellow tulips and looked at them in dismay, letting them drop. He offered Eva a lone, bent, shredded tulip. She took it with a diverted smile as she turned to remove her hat and the enormous white feather boa that encircled her neck and hung to the ground.

"Thank you – that's nice," she said. Her lips twitched.

"I'm sorry . . . I'm very sorry . . ." Paul mumbled.

Her lips tilted and she looked directly at him. He felt faint again. "Is that your bottle blocking the entrance?"

Paul outlined the bottle with his hands. Eva nodded. He looked sheepish. He thought he would deny it, and changed his mind.

"Yes – it's my bottle."

"Would you move it away please?" she said with a charming gesture.

Paul nodded helplessly and edged out of the room like a shy and very small boy. He leaned against the outside door and looked at the bottle with loathing. Where would he put it? He picked it up and staggered to the stairs and promptly fell down them.

In her room Eva listened to the crash, an amused smile playing about her mouth. She noticed that her silver-framed photograph had been moved and she picked it up, looking thoughtfully towards the door, beyond which could be heard the distant sounds of Paul and his bottle rolling down the stairs.

Paul day-dreamed about Eva that night before he dropped off to sleep, and then he dreamed about her again. She was so cool and languid and beautiful. Like a tall, slender, remote goddess. Once he had been destined to be a hero, a god, and if things had been different, he could have won her ... but now, he was a bottle. He would have to do something great – but what? His dreams gave him no answers.

On the opposite side of the well Cilly stared out of her window towards Paul's room. The stars were very bright and the moon was high, but the beams were shining in to her own room and Paul's was dark and desirable. She took off her warm, sensible pyjamas and dressed herself in a skimpy garment of peach coloured satin then pulled on a warm dressing gown. She had her mother's key to the Prygodski flat and slipped in like a ghost and paused. The flat was full of strange noises and she listened, trying to identify them.

From some of the rooms came deep sighs and giggles and furtive creaks. The whores, she supposed, still hard at it. Then she saw Mutti creep along the passage and enter Major von Mueller's room directly opposite where Cilly was standing. The curtains were drawn, but there was a gap, and the moonlight flooded in and Cilly could see in. Mutti slipped her hands beneath the blankets where von Mueller lay in a deep, snoring sleep and removed something.

Cilly could not see what it was until Mutti was back in the passage and she stared with some amazement at a hot water bottle. Mutti was looking very pleased with herself. She entered the Colonel's room, leaving the door ajar. Not meaning to spy, but very curious, Cilly crept along and peered through the gap. The Colonel was bolt upright in his chair, his eyes wide open staring directly at Cilly. She felt a shiver up her spine and nearly backed away.

Mutti tucked the hot water bottle at her husband's feet.

She spoke softly, crooningly. "Everyone's talking about losing the war, but no one seems to remember that we've lost our youth. I think of all the years I spent polishing your boots, your medals . . ."

The Colonel's face seemed not to move, but to Cilly his expression seemed to gain in terror. He looked petrified.

She fled silently along the carpeted passage to Paul's room. She opened the door and stood leaning against it. Paul was in a deep sleep, his breathing regular. She moved towards the foot of the bed, near the window. The moon had shifted and a beam fell through the window lighting a small portion of the corner of the bed. Paul was still in the shadows.

Cilly slowly removed her robe, and stood in her skimpy satin pyjama top. Her breasts were outlined and tipped in silver, and a silver radiance ran down her left thigh and calf, leaving her belly and pubic mound in shadow. She shook the bed and Paul rolled over in fright, tangling with his sheets. His eyes sprang open.

He saw Cilly at the foot of his bed and for a moment he didn't know who she was. He had been dreaming about Eva, and he thought he was still dreaming. Then he saw it was Cilly. One nude leg was propped on his bed, and she was sensuously massaging it with her hands as if she were stroking a giant penis.

Paul felt threatened.

"I have nice legs, don't I?" she said softly, provocatively.

Paul turned on the light and the dream-like atmosphere, the sheen of the moon on silk skin and satin, was gone.

"Cilly."

"In person."

She stood on the bed, then jumped on Paul playfully. He remained rigid. Cilly nibbled the lobe of his ear, and murmured theatrically, "Imagine you're now at the front. Blood, horror, explosion . . ." she looked to see the effect of her words, but Paul appeared unmoved. She continued, warming to her theme. "And a little soldier's whore comes to warm you up . . ." she snuggled closer to Paul . . . ". . . and you take her slowly . . . as you would sip a cup of tea . . ."

Paul was startled. "A cup of tea?"

"Well ... coffe then." She wished Paul would play the game, but refused to admit defeat.

"When I was a little girl I imagined that you would take me like some great crusader . . . you'd return on a white horse . . . make love to me on the floor . . . in a boat . . . on horseback ... in the centre of the city ...". she clutched Paul enthusiastically "On the Victory Monument!"

"There was no victory," Paul said flatly.

"Aren't you being sentimental? Didn't they teach you how to kill?"

"Not really." He glanced down his nose at her. "And you're behaving like an actress, like some sex-starved, undisciplined, immoral slut."

Cilly giggled. "I certainly hope so."

There was no reaction from Paul. He lay like a log. Cilly ground her teeth together in a rage and sat up, pushing her tumbled curls back. Paul thought how pretty and how uninteresting she looked.

"It's no good – it's not getting me anywhere, is it? Oh Paul, just imagine we're in Venice. On a gondola. Somebody's serenading us as we're going down the canals oh, can't you get just a little bit romantic?"

She noticed that his eyes were fixed beyond her at something far away.

"What are you looking at, darling?"

"The stars."

Paul got out of bed in his crisp blue pyjamas and walked to the window. Cilly got up slowly and looked at his perfect profile. She sighed and pulled on her dressing gown.

"I'd forgotten how beautiful they are in Germany."

"And that's not the only thing you've forgotten," Cilly said bitterly.

Paul ignored her and opened the windows. They stepped out onto the balcony and Paul stared silently, almost reverently up at the spangled vault above him. It was, he realised, the first time that he had seen the sky since the war. It had been covered with clouds, so it seemed to him, since a month or more before the final explosion. The battlefield had been full of dust, and heavy with snow clouds. He had no recollection of the year in France, and since his return to

Berlin everything had been gloomy, depressed and cloudy. And now, here, at last was the universe exposed.

"Yes, the stars are shining brightly tonight," Cilly said as if she were quoting from one of her songs. She looked at Paul as she leaned against him, "but you, my little warrior, are suffering from shell shock."

She stepped along the balcony a little way and peered over. "Well, I tried." She turned again to look at Paul; and now she had his attention. She felt very sad. "But just keep looking up there ... someday you might see another beautiful German star ..." She walked to the door and smiled furiously. "... Me!" Then she was gone.

Paul seemed scarcely to notice her going. He remained dreamily gazing into space, thinking of Eva. She was so close – just a few yards away in his father's old study. He could walk out of his door, knock on her door, and be in her room, her languid eyes fixed on his face in her mocking way.

The well below opened on one side onto a small park, and a movement caught Paul's eye. It was Eva. For a moment, because he had been thinking about her so intensely, he thought it was a vision, then he saw her dogs were pulling her along with their great, loping gallop. She was leaning back in a curiously elegant way, looking not at all flustered by the pace at which they moved.

A tall, elderly man stepped forward. He had obviously been waiting for her. He bowed, and touched her familiarly. She smiled and allowed it. He bowed again.

"Tomorrow, at this time," he said. "I look forward to it with pleasure."

Paul could not hear her low reply. The man walked rapidly away, and Eva glanced up. Her eyes locked with Paul's, then he ducked out of sight and almost fell back into his room. He felt faint again, and very cold.

He lay on his bed shaking and weeping. So – she was a whore; like all the others. Even like Cilly. Even like his own mother.

Cilly lay on her bed across the well and also wept, not in pain, but in mortification.

Paul decided he would ignore Eva, but every time he

passed her door the next day he trembled and paused. Then, there she was at the front door to the flat as he came past on another unnecessary errand. She was receiving a great pile of beautifully wrapped packages. She staggered under the weight and turned to see Paul watching her.

"Would you be so kind, Paul as to help me with these? Sorry – I simply couldn't manage them myself."

Paul came forward and stood dutifully as she loaded them into his arms. She smiled faintly, and like a mist her subtle perfume drifted over his swelling head. He felt his penis move, like a little live creature at her closeness, and the blood also rushed to his head. He had never felt like this before. No woman had ever affected him like this before – it was as if his own body were not under his control.

He stood rigidly wondering if she knew; if her perfume contained some strange aphrodisiac. He tried to think of her with other men; tried to think of her as a whore, but she was so beautiful so elegant, so distant, that it was impossible, and all the while he grew harder. The harder he grew, the more rigidly he controlled himself until his expression was icy and his spine tense.

Eva sensed his imposed distance and she went out of her way to be charming. She smiled as she led the way to her room and opened the door.

"Thank you – put them just there."

Paul moved to where she indicated and the dogs rose. He paused.

"Sit . . . sit . . ." she said. She turned back to Paul. "Won't you stay a minute?"

"I'm really rather busy." Shortly. "Sorry."

"Please." Meltingly. "Please – won't you sit down?"

"Very well."

"A little tea perhaps?"

She came close to him, smiling softly. She always seemed to him to be far away, as if not in this world, yet she was the most sensuous woman he had ever met.

He looked at her longingly, trying to keep his features a mask. She wore a beaded black velvet coat of great elegance. The sleeves were wide and the back swung away from her slender body in a wide pleat. Her lovely swan's neck was framed in the collar, which was padded and pleated with oyster satin, like the shell on which Aphrodite rose from the foam in all her glory.

This was getting ridiculous he was getting poetic and sentimental. he might be a bottle, but he was also a Prussian, and sentiment did not run in his family.

The dogs reared up and broke his train of thought.

"No! No!" she said crossly. "Please. Sit! Sit!"

"If they're such a nuisance, why don't you get rid of them?"

She laughed, lifting her eyebrows. She had a deep and ravishing dimple at the corner of her mouth. Paul stared at it longingly.

"Oh no, I couldn't possibly do that." She set out the tea things with a delicate touch, glancing up at him. She paused. "Gifts from old lovers must always be kept, no matter how cumbersome." Her eyes met Paul's and their gaze locked. She continued the speak while staring into his eyes as if the words scarcely mattered. "Sometimes I think the larger the gift, the more ineffective the lover ..."

At the word lover, Paul dropped his gaze then looked up again. This time his eyes looked at her accusingly.

"Why are you looking at me like that?" she asked, knowing the reason.

"I saw you last night!"

She spoke slowly and coolly, distantly, as if it were no business of his. "You're a soldier. An officer. Berlin is not the place for soldiers now. People only want to forget the war. I too, had hopes . I had ambitions ..." she shrugged. "But, as you see ..."

"Aren't you ashamed?"

She was amused. "Ashamed? Shame belongs to another decade. There is no such thing today." She looked at him directly. "Your bottle —" Paul flushed and she smiled. "You shouldn't be ashamed of your bottle, either. It's a wonderful hiding place until you find yourself."

Paul was startled and touched by her perception. He started to laugh – a real laugh for the first time in many years.

"See ..." she said gaily. "You can laugh! You should do it more often. It becomes you."

Paul stopped laughing and they looked intently at each other. He moved his hands in a small gesture, and a small sigh escaped. "Do you think it will ever be the same again?" He hear his question from a distance, like a mocking echo. "Do you think it will ever be the same again?"

"No. It will *never* be the same again."

* * * * *

SIX

Paul still had not grown used to his bottle. He staggered down the street in it, waving from side to side so that passers-by had to give him a wide berth, or even, cross the street. At times the momentum of his stagger would spin him right round, and rather than fight to turn back, he would walk back the way he had just come. On a windy day he often traversed the same stretch many times like a wildly spinning top.

Major von Mueller emerged from a pissoir and mockingly raised his homburg. "Morning, Paul."

"How did you know it was me?" came the muffled sound from deep in the belly of the bottle.

"Shouldn't think I would fail to recognise the contents of *any* bottle at fifty paces." He tapped the bottle playfully. "Isn't this a little undignified?"

"Certainly ... inconvenient. Excuse me." Paul wavered his way to the entrance of the pissoir and attempted to enter. The bottle jammed, and he fought to free himself while von Mueller watched shaking his head.

"Oh God," Paul said dolefully. He had visions of pee running down his legs – the bottle leaking as he walked along the street.

"You know, I really think you should consider my influence – let me help you," von Mueller said as Paul staggered back. There had been a ripping sound. If the bottle were damaged he would probably lose his wages. "I have a friend ..." von Mueller continued. "You should meet him ... he's looking for dedicated young officers like you, loyal to the Fatherland. Yes, certainly you should meet him."

Paul had been directed by von Mueller to a huge seedy hall with a concrete floor and big, dusty windows. There was a slanted concrete track in the form of a circle, surrounded by wooden benches. A boxing ring was in the centre of the circle. The whole area appeared to be filled with the crippled, the handicapped, the limbless.

Wounded soldiers didn't fade away – they all congregated

here, in this derelict place, Paul thought as he watched the legless whizz past him in small carts, like children's soap boxes, and the armless – or at least, the one-armed, prance about a boxing-ring, attacking each other with the one good arm each had.

Paul stopped the trainer. He felt very timid before all these genuine wounded heroes. "Excuse me, von Mueller sent me."

The trainer glared at him, as if affronted by the sight of a whole man.

"I know who sent you!" he jerked his head. "The boss is up there!"

Paul waited until the cart race had passed him. The legless were using wooden blocks to propel themselves along the track. Above them, on a cat-walk, a man stood watching morosely. Paul approached him cautiously.

"Excuse me, Major von Mueller sent me . . ."

The man turned and glared ferociously at Paul, who stared back at him incredulously.

The brief image focused, then was printed on his mind, of the Captain cartwheeling through the air after the explosion of the final shell of the war. He had thought he was dead.

"Captain?" Paul clicked his heels almost religiously.

"Who?"

"Przygodski, Sir."

"Przygodski . . . ?"

"Sir!"

Recognition dawned. "But you were in the war, weren't you?"

Yes, Sir."

"Gott in Himmel! You were in the war!"

Paul smiled boyishly. "Yes Sir, that's right Sir."

The Captain looked stunned. "You're still alive?"

Yes, Sir. I'm ready for duty – Sir!"

Captain Kraft approached Paul, his eyes on fire. "It's very good to have you back." He put his arms round Paul and held him close for a moment.

"It's very good to be back, Sir."

"We didn't lose the war, did we?" the Captain asked eagerly.

"No, Sir!"

"And we'll win the peace, won't we?"

Paul clicked his heels, fired with a fresh enthusiasm. "Sir!"

They started to walk backwards and forwards along the cat walk while the strange games continued below.

"We have a great deal to accomplish," the Captain said. He extended his hands to take in the stadium and the streets beyond. "Do you realise that the future of Germany lies in these hands?" He whirled round and held them out to Paul.

"Yes. Yes, Sir – yes!"

Herman closed his strong hands round Paul's slender and aristocratically shaped ones and glared into his eyes, his face inches away. Paul did not feel that he were mad – rather that he were lit with an inner flame; a burning zeal.

"You may have a chance to share my balcony when we unite our people," the Captain said movingly. "Follow me!"

They marched to a derelict U Bahn shaft not far from the stadium and the Captain led the way down some damp, dingy steps littered with old newspapers and the dank smell of disuse and decay. It was dark, lit only by the occasional vent, so that they moved from patches of dark and light with few grey areas.

The Captain's voice echoed in the shaft as he continued his soliloquy. He was still holding tightly to one of Paul's hands. His vice-like grip was painful, but Paul didn't want to ask him to release it. It was unlikely that the Captain was aware he was still holding on to him.

"I'll show you some things, my boy, that will change the entire course of your life. We have the chance to realise the dreams and ambitions of our forefathers – to rid our society of the avarice and crime of our times. The thought – the actual thought – that some people have that war can be abolished, can be banished from the world is not only absurd – but it involves the atrophy of some of the finest, essential, things of mankind!"

Paul tried to follow this logic – that war was necessary; but the pain in his hand grew unbearable. "Captain Kraft – my hand – it hurts."

"Yes, but it hurts me too, when I think of our Fatherland overrun by vermin," the Captain said entirely illogically but not understanding Paul's complaint.

He did not let go of Paul's hand, but dragged him relentlessly on into the depths until they reached the heart of the U Bahn system and they dived along a track and into a siding where an old abandoned U Bahn car stood. The car had been transformed into the Captain's living quarters. Paul was amazed to see that next to the car were mountains of crates of live ammunition. He looked at them and turned to the Captain – "Where did all this come from? Aren't the tracks ever checked?"

"We control most things that you aren't aware of yet," the Captain said triumphantly as he slid back the door of the car and hauled Paul inside. He waved at the rather grim, lice infested interior, dominated by the huge horn of a gramophone and piles of books tumbled in wild confusion.

"Over the hill, and into battle! Well, what do you think of it – it's wonderful, isn't it?"

Paul's smile was rather forced. He wasn't sure now, what was happening, or even, if the Captain were sane.

The Captain picked up the volumes near a military type cot converted from three seats and tossed them to Paul one at a time, jerking out the titles as he did so.

"Nietzsche . . . Clausewitz . . . Goethe . . ."

Paul valiantly fielded the heavy tomes which were in danger of knocking him out. "You've read all these?" he gasped, winded.

"Read? I don't have time to read!" The Captain said, scandalised.

The Captain cranked the handle of the gramophone. "No, I don't have time to read – others do that for me . . . the books are there for inspiration. Do you like music?" Paul had no time to answer. "Listen to this! Listen!" The Captain grinned triumphantly. "Do you recognise it?"

Paul strained his ears to the distorted disc but before he could answer, the Captain came to his rescue. "Wagner – 'Ring de Nibelungen'!" He waved his arms heroically in time to the scratchy rhythm, not of the music, but of the wobbling disc, walking the length of the car in his eager strides. He turned and looked closely at Paul and nodded.

"I see it now . . masses of blond-haired, blue-eyed

subjects with our names on their lips and our beliefs in their hearts waiting for us to give them that great idea . . ."

"What idea?"

"I don't know it yet!" he said, looking slightly confused, then turned and charged to the end of the car and through it to another compartment. His voice came from a distance.

"People are working on it . . . but we must let nothing stand in our way . . . especially women!"

"Women?" Paul said, dazed.

The Captain re-appeared, his face contorted. "Do you realise that a passionate woman can destroy the greatest warrior! Do you remember what Josephine did to Napoleon?"

"What?"

Herman dived closer as if to tell a great secret. "She . . ." he drew in his breath. "What does it matter. We are re-writing history. From here we shall spread tentacles of our organisation through every street in this city!" his voice raised. "Propaganda – with propaganda, through every city in this country and through every country in the world!"

He paused at the glorious image and a train shot by on the tracks, rocking the car and blowing all the papers in the air in wild confusion. He and Paul dived for the papers and tried to hold them down. Eventually the wind passed. The Captain arranged the papers in neat piles, and Paul appreciated that they meant nothing at all; were there to give the semblance of a working HQ.

The Captain glanced at the restored order in satisfaction.

"You can stay here, if you want," he said to Paul.

Paul was moved. "Thank you very much," he said.

The days started to fall into a routine. It was like being on manoeuvres in the subterranean heart of the city instead of in the Hertz Mountains. The stadium and the U Bahn became the focus of his days and nights. He boxed with the limbless and ran circuits with burly young men who spent their days spewing out their hatred of the Communists. Until then, Paul, from his Prussian heights, had barely heard the word; but these were men of the masses and they knew.

At night, before he dropped off to sleep, Paul thought of

Eva with a perfect longing. He didn't want to sleep with her, but wanted to worship at her feet. It was for her and women like her, that he wanted to restore the German Empire. Honourable women whom the fortunes of war had misused, abused and degraded. Good German women who wore the tatty clothes of French whores; and he was the Prince who was to restore their pride.

When he thought in that way, in the limbo between sleep and wakefulness, his own pride grew and nourished. But generally speaking, when he was honest with himself, he found himself wondering what it was all about. His admiration for the Captain – whom he now called Herman – was tinged with the growing conviction that he was mad. He tried to smother this conviction and it didn't particularly worry him. His whole life since he had been blown up, had had an insane, bizarre quality that made him take each day as it came without too much rationalisation. Now that the Empire had been swept away nothing made sense anyway.

Paul lay on the cot in the U Bahn car, his thoughts in a jumble of the past and the unreal present, through which images of Eva drifted like a star seen through the mists of Autumn. The contorted music of Wagner filled the small space with the essence of its own insanity.

A burly young man in an assortment of regimental clothes suddenly appeared at one end of the car and glared with all the malignant hatred of a Caliban at Paul.

"You swine!" he ground out, between clenched teeth.

Paul's eye flew open. The young man looked so ferocious that Paul's fears multiplied. "I beg your pardon?" he said politely.

The intruder suddenly lunged at him and Paul rolled out of his reach, while the stranger crashed into the gramophone. He turned and glowered at Paul.

"You're certainly pretty. Pretty enough," he said, and light began to dawn on Paul. He started to laugh. The man was jealous! Jealous of him and Herman.

"You swine!" The stranger repeated and launched himself again at Paul, knocking the huge trumpet of the gramophone. The needle slipped once more as fresh scratches were dug into the wavy disc.

"You've ruined it!" Paul protested. He stood erect in his pretty pyjamas. "And if you wish to address me, you'll do so correctly. My name is Lieutenant Paul Ambrosius Pryzgodski."

"Ambrosius!" The stranger glowered. The name filled him with more loathing, determined now that Paul must indeed be Herman's pretty boy. "I'll show you!"

Before Paul could move, the man lunged at him in a fury and bopped him firmly on the nose with such force that Paul crashed back into the pile of classical books stacked up for Herman's inspiration.

"By nobe ib broken!" Paul howled.

"Otto!"

The Captain loomed in the entrance to the car. His frown was cold and his expression forbidding.

Otto fell awkwardly off Paul and cringed in the corner, while Paul stumbled to his feet and moved closer to the protection of the Captain.

"Paul, would you leave us please. Go outside, if you will. Right outside."

"I . . . I . . . No! No!" whimpered Otto.

Paul looked at him stunned. The man was a great brute, bigger by far than the Captain, yet he was cringing like a small child. Still holding his nose Paul half fell out of the car into the dark tunnel, dimly illuminated by the lights from the car's shuttered windows.

"No . . . please . . ." he heard Otto sob, then he heard the heavy violence of beating. "Forgive me, Herman, forgive me . . . I forgot myself . . . I didn't mean "

The beating continued. Presently Herman left the car and sat on one of the crates of ammunition next to Paul. They sat in silence for a while, then the Captain put his arm about Paul and gave him a slight squeeze.

"Sorry about this Paul. Otto's nerves are shattered . . . shot to pieces . . . the pressures of terrorism."

He dragged at his cigarette. Paul noticed that his hand was trembling.

"He'll be staying with us for a while – you won't mind? Just until he's himself again." He looked at Paul pathetically.

"I hope you didn't attach too much importance to what he said ... what he did ... we mustn't let trivialities stand in our way." He looked directly at Paul over the glowing end of his cigarette as he drew deeply on it. "Must we?"

* * * * *

SEVEN

It was Christmas. The magnificent goose, white feathers as clean as fresh snow, yellow beak as bright as a daffodil, was on the kitchen table in the flat. Beside it lay a long, sharply pointed dagger.

"You kill the goose," Hilda said, "And I'll make the stuffing."

"No . . . no . . . no . . ." Mutti said faintly.

The goose stretched its sleek, strong neck and surveyed the kitchen in disgust. It's feet were solid and orange.

"Why?"

"No, *you* kill the goose and *I'll* make the stuffing," Mutti decided.

"No, no, no, no. You kill the goose and I'll make the stuffing."

"No – I want to make the stuffing!"

"No!"

They both stared at the goose who grew larger and stronger and more solidly alive by the minute. Hilda snatched up the knife and made a move. "You're so helpless!"

The goose stretched his neck and hissed. Mutti clapped her hand to her mouth. "No . . . no . . . you mustn't."

Hilda poised over the goose while Mutti fluttered hopelessly.

"What *are* you doing?"

Mutti dropped her hand from her mouth and turned. "Paul!"

"Merry Christmas, Mutti." He walked a little into the hall and beckoned Captain Kraft to enter the kitchen.

"Mother, this is Captain Kraft! Aunt Hilda, Captain Kraft!"

Hilda and Mutti removed their aprons and patted their hair, smiling foolishly and moistly at Paul whom they hadn't see for some time.

"Please; please come in," Mutti said. "I'm so glad that you could come. I had the feeling that Paul was trying to hide you from us . . ." Paul laughed and shook his head, raising his brow at Herman. "I'm so glad that he is enjoying his new position with you – such a good job!"

"Paul is one in a million," Herman said seriously.

"Yes, he is!" Mutti beamed affectionately at both of them. She turned back to the goose. "You must excuse us, but we are just trying to slaughter . . ." she winced.

"Perhaps I can be of some assistance?" Herman said smoothly.

"Yes, would you please? That would be so kind of you . . ."

Herman scooped the goose into his arms, and, holding it close against his belted leather coat, took it off into the kitchen. Mutti and Hilda closed their eyes and uttered faint shrieks of protest.

The goose hissed and attempted to peck at the Captain's swastika tie-clip, but Herman caught it firmly by the neck and plunged it head first into the sink full of water. Its squawking was cut off at once.

Herman allowed a faint smile to cross his face. "I may not eat meat," he said, "but I do know something about animals."

The table was laid, the silver polished, the crystal sparkling. Meats and fruits, nuts, cakes in silver dishes, jellies, sausages, pates. It was quite like old times.

The Colonel sat at the head of the long, snowy-clothed table, staring sightlessly ahead, and the family and guests watched Mutti as she carved the golden, crisp-skinned goose.

Herman raised his glass. "I would like to say that the Colonel's contribution to the war will not be forgotten."

Paul clapped. "Hear, hear!"

Von Mueller lifted his glass and sipped from it, bowing at Eva. "Nor will the contribution of Miss Eva . . . such good wine."

Eva glanced at Paul with a faint smile then turned sarcastically to Herman. She spoke directly at him. "I thought I'd donate it to help celebrate Paul's new life." She paused and her tone grew malicious. "They tell me you don't eat meat?"

She picked at a small piece of goose from the serving dish and popped it delicately into her mouth, watching Herman all the time.

"Not a bite!" Herman said proudly, her sarcasm going over his head.

"Do you abstain for religious reasons or are you just a mystic by nature?"

"The only religious abstentions I have are from religion," Herman said.

Cilly hooted, tossing her curls and rolling her eyes dramatically. "That sounds like a line out of Vaudeville . . . 'Ya know what I gave up for Lent . . . ? Religion!' " She looked at Herman and hesitated at his furious expression. "No, no, I take it back . . . I'm sorry . . . it lacks taste."

"God died in this country, my dear," Herman said, as if to a child.

Cilly resented his tone. "Really? That must have been some funeral."

"Please Cilly," said Mutti, "It's not one of your shows . . ."

"Shows? You're the one who invited all the clowns," Cilly said rudely. She laughed, the strong wine had gone straight to her head. "I thought this was anybody's show isn't it?"

"Cilly!" Paul said.

Herman stood up. "It's all right, Paul. We in command have to suffer greater hazards than the idle conversation of women."

"Oh? Do you think you know a great deal about *women*, Captain?" Eva said with meaning.

"Excuse me!" Herman stalked to the door, followed by Paul.

"Oh, Captain Kraft . . ." Mutti quavered, getting up to restrain the Captain. She glanced around the table at the unrepentant faces. "Well . . ." she said doubtfully.

"Please come again soon, some time . . . you know where we are."

"Yes, I know *exactly* where you all are."

"I'll see you later, Herman," Paul said humbly, as he helped the Captain on with his coat. Herman nodded and touched Paul on the arm. He looked deeply hurt.

Paul returned to the dining room and glanced coldly at the

now sheepish faces.

"Paul, I'm sorry," Eva said.

Paul ignored her. He bowed to his mother. "Please excuse me, Mother," he said stiffly.

Paul slammed the door and ran down the steps towards the exit. He heard the door bang again, but kept on moving.

"Wait, Paul, wait," Cilly called, but Paul turned his collar up against the night and marched stoically on. Cilly caught him up and tucked her hand in his arm.

"Come on, Paul. You've been gone for months at least you could tell us where you live."

"Please! Cilly, it's none of your business. Not now."

"Oh, come on Paul we might not see you again for ages"

"I can't tell you it's a military secret."

"But what about us your family . . . friends . . . *me*?"

Paul stopped and turned to face her. She looked very cold in her evening frock. "Cilly, there comes a time in every man's life when he has to avoid making the same mistakes as . . . as Napoleon."

"Paul," Cilly said firmly, "You're slipping off the deep end again."

"Not at all. It's just that, finally, I'm coming very close to my lifelong purpose."

"What purpose?"

"I'm not sure yet." Cilly stared at him in amazement. "That is, people round here are taking notes . . . that is, I mean, Herman isn't quite as clear as he ought to be . . ."

"Herman isn't the only one!"

Paul ignored her. ". . . but he hasn't given up like everyone else."

Cilly shook her head. "Shell shock. It's got to be shell-shock." She kissed him and turned and skipped back down the street, like a wind-blown flower.

Paul stared after her, wondering why she was suddenly so happy. He turned to see Herman hunched into his collar under a tree, waiting for him.

"Herman, I'm sorry . . ." he said when he reached him. Herman glared at him, then slapped him very hard across the face. Paul rode the slap like a boxer, then became rigid. He glared back at Herman, not in fury, but in icy contempt. At once Herman melted.

"Paul . . . Paul . . . I'm sorry."

"I need no rich man's plenty . . . they're always seventy . . . a Lieutenant around twenty . . . is good enough – for me!" sang Cilly as she postured before the huge baroque mirror in the rehearsal room. She turned, one hand on her hip, stretching her black-stockinged leg towards the small audience. A transvestite with smooth black hair, carefully made up face and directoire knickers, his stockings rolled down to his knees, stared hard at Paul, his tongue making little flickers of desire.

". . . I'm restless like a sailor . . . don't want to be confined by any rich old gaoler . . . a Lieutenant around twenty is good enough . . . good enough . . . to fall in love with me . . ."

She smiled at Paul, who had sat through her performance like David, as if carved from a piece of marble.

"Hi!" she said, as she stood before him, legs apart, hands on hips.

"Shall I ask for your autograph?"

"Well . . . well . . . I believed you were definitely lost. I explained to everyone that you showed up every third year." She smiled at him with affection.

"Everybody – at home – happy, then?"

"Sure, they're happy. Unhappiness is out of fashion now! We're all reborn – regilded! No one has the right to say they were born under an unlucky star."

They stared at each other a long moment. Cilly felt moved to the point of tears.

"Come on, get your coat," she said gaily. "I've got a couple of hours before the next show."

* * * * *

EIGHT

Two hats walked down the street. One was fluttering with feathers, the other had a fox skin dangling from the brim. Berlin, five years after the war seemed to have more colour, more warmth. The worms had crept out of the woodwork and society was firmly divided into a new order of the haves and have nots.

Fra von Putzdorf sighed theatrically. "It's so sad having to celebrate the Kaiser's birthday when he's in exile!"

"I have a picture of him chopping wood in Doorn " said Frau von Uexkull.

"How brave of him doing something so dangerous . . . He could have hurt himself!" They each sighed sentimentally.

"My husband says that this is actually war-time camouflaged as peace," Frau von Uexkull said after a pause, in which they had both remembered how it had been before. "What won't the Kaiser think of next!"

"The truth is, you know that some people lost and some gained from the war . . . why, just look at Wilhelmina von Przygodski! She found this Major von . . . whatever his name is . . ."

"Mueller."

"Yes, that's it. Major von Meuller. You know, my dear, the minute he moved in, they seemed to have everything. Everything!" Frau von Putzdorf nodded. "The tea they have is so good!"

"I heard there was this freighter filled with tea that was smuggled from Shanghai to Hamburg and he told me once that . . ." their voices faded as they reached the von Przygodski building and started to climb the stairs, panting. They, too, obviously were not deprived of nutrition.

The Kaiser's birthday party was in full swing in the von Przygodski apartment. Major von Mueller appeared to be acting as proxy host for the Colonel, who was dressed in his best uniform and all his medals. "Good afternoon, good afternoon ladies," he cried, and, almost immediately as the bell rang again, "Excuse me, ladies . . ." He dived down the passage.

"So nice to see you," cooed Frau von Putzdorf as she peered to see what there was to eat.

"Lovely hats you both have!" from Mutti who patted her blonde curls anxiously.

"Actually, they're quite different, you know," said Frau von Putzdorf. "I'm not sure where Maria got *hers*, but I picked this little thing up at . . ."

"Frau von Kaisering!" Major von Mueller announced.

"Frau von Kaisering!" the two hats bobbed in awed tones as if the Kaiserin herself had walked in.

"Helga, my dear!" said Mutti.

Frau von Kaisering looked very beautiful in her dark cream coat with a brown mink hem. A fine veil covered her golden page-boy bob. She threw the veil back and smiled mistily at the assembled guests. Her voice was low and husky. "I'm sorry, dear friends . . . I've had a slight mishap . . . my husband, the General . . . he died of a stroke this morning."

Complete silence followed.

"But Helga!" Mutti finally protested. "That's terrible! He was so healthy."

"Yes, I know," Helga's smile trembled. "Poor man – all his life he wanted to die with a bullet!" There was a sudden flicker from the Colonel's rigid eyes, but no one noticed as Frau von Kaisering continued, "But we can't always have what we want, can we?"

Major von Mueller coughed. "I propose we have a moment of silence to commemorate the departure of a man who was a fine, fine soldier."

Hilda turned to the Colonel, who was again staring sightlessly ahead. She shouted in his ear, "We're going to have a moment of silence, Gustav, for Helga's husband."

They all bowed and stood staring thoughfully at the Persian carpet. There was a sudden crash and clatter as Paul fell through the salon doors. He picked himself up and looked at the elegant group in bewilderment. Helga von Kaisering, who had been standing closest to the doors, with her back to them, slowly turned her head and looked at Paul. He stared back at her. In looks they were a curious reflection of each other. It was almost as if they were looking into a mirror and each recognised what they saw. Helga smiled slowly and with anticipation.

"My son," said Mutti.

* * * * *

NINE

The grey and red of the senior officer's uniforms made a bright splash among the black weeds of the civilian mourners. Their faces were uneasy though they tried not to show apprehension as the sound of staccato gunfire drew nearer. The crackle of firearms was at odds with the stiff, mournful throb of the big drum leading the band.

They stood around like people waiting for a dull party to begin. The signal for the festivities was the coffin as it was brought out, borne by the pallbearers and led by the vicar. By the side of the catafalque, serious, seemingly sad and extremely sexy, came the General's widow.

Mutti and Aunt Hilda almost felt they were back in the old days as they watched, on either side of the Colonel's chair. The Colonel neither saw nor heard nor gave any sign of interest in the proceedings.

"Isn't it a shame that Gustav can't be here to enjoy this?" Hilda said. Mutti tried to hush her. "No, you know what I mean. He is here, of course, but really he isn't ..." Again Mutti tried to hush her though whether for deference for the dead dead or the living dead, even she was not sure. "... But he isn't is he? – What a way to go, like a hero!"

Hilda had lost Mutti. "Who's going?" she asked. "Who's a hero?"

"The General of course. What a hero! Paul should follow in his footsteps!"

"Why? Why should Paul follow in his footsteps?"

There was another burst of rifle fire and the sound of bullets richocheting off marble tombs, and the footsteps Hilda was talking about began to speed up just a fraction. Paul, sensing a danger he had not felt during his minutes on a battlefield, dropped back from the main body of mourners to walk alongside his mother.

"Mutti, whoever they are, they seem to be getting closer. Perhaps you should go back now," he said.

"Nonsense," she said, firmly. "These idiots from who knows where – they don't even respect the dead. But go back? Never!" And as if following the same line of thought and remembering which idiots she was talking about, she asked: "How's it going with Captain Kraft, by the way?"

The firing was even closer and Paul thought that soon bullets would be going over their heads: "Not very well, Mutti. You know, despite being comrades in arms, we really don't have very much in common."

From the corner of his eye, Paul could now see that there were men over by the cemetery wall. But apart from the slight quickening of pace, nothing had so far disturbed the body of mourners. They set their faces with Prussian stoicism and were not to be frightened off by armed madmen. Even so, little signs of tension were creeping through – the twitching of mouths, the tensing of muscles ready to hurl their bodies forward.

Paul looked at Helga von Kaisering and thought it odd that she seemed to have noticed nothing. Her attention seemed to be only for him. Her widows weeds, her lilies, the flag-covered coffin in which her husband lay, the quickening pace and mounting hysteria: all this seemed not to have touched her. He wondered why.

The vicar, in good clerical fashion, was the first to put the panic into words. He looked over his shoulder and whispered fiercely to the pallbearers: "Faster! Faster!" in the hope that when the coffin moved forward at speed, everything else would as well.

The gallant officers bearing the General's earthly remains needed little exhortation. The coffin began to move down the path like a battering ram and the pace they set quickly thinned out the field of elderly mourners. Most of the ladies, seeing the coffin leap ahead and feeling even more exposed, beat a hasty retreat to the chapel. The most senior and gaga of the officers seeing the dissolution all around him had faint memories of manoeuvres under the crippled Kaiser and gave a wavering order to form to the left. Unfortunately, in this case, the formation left the main body of mourners without the presence of military men – they were all charging ahead with the coffin – and a whimpering panic followed.

"Oh, please come back," Hilda called after them to no avail. In front, the pastor and his flock had broken into a sheepish trot and the pallbearers, unmindful of their dignified load, did the same. The downhill path made it all too easy for Mutti and Hilda to move the Colonel at speed and soon the chair was pulling away from them.

Now the crack of rifle shots was immediately followed by the whine of bullets just over the party's heads. Mutti was beside herself and called on her husband, in his carved and tapestry-covered chair, to slow down, but her call went unanswered

"Mutti, you must go back to the chapel, quickly," Paul said.

"Not unless you come with us," she answered, but at that moment the widow came alongside Paul and slipped her arm through his

"I must stay with the coffin and need an officer to protect me," she breathed.

"The crypt," said Paul. "We'll be safe in the crypt. Don't worry, Mutti, I'll get her to safety," he called over his shoulder, and they began to spring after the vanishing coffin, leaving a protesting Mutti and Hilda behind. Then Mutti, blind to everything but the danger of flying bullets, forgot everything and fled for her life, while Hilda dived into a thicket of ferns and peered fearfully over the top of a tombstone.

The coffin was heading at breakneck speed for the open crypt when one of the warring party's bullets smashed into it, splintering the veneered oak and leaving a gaping hole. Suddenly it lurched through the open door of the crypt and shot under its own momentum down the stairs as if on skis as the attendant officers gave up the unequal struggle between the dignity of the occasion and terror of the occasional. Even before it was on its way into its final resting place the stout men and true took to their heels and ran.

Paul pushed Frau von Kaisering in after the coffin and threw himself after her. He didn't see the look of triumph on the beautiful widow's face.

They fell on the floor of the crypt in a welter of crushed lilies, the German flag tangled round their limbs as it slid slowly off the battered coffin. The widow looked with awe at the gaping hole smashed in the wood: "Look!" she said. "Look at the coffin! He got his hero's bullet after all." And then her face softened as she became aware of the intimacy of the situation and she changed roles. "Oh thank you, Lieutenant, thank you. I don't know what I would have done without you."

They rose to their feet and took a step closer. Paul couldn't take his eyes from her face. She was soft and desirable like a sexy choirboy in her tailored black coat and veil, the candles glinting on her hair and making dark shadows of her eyes, glistening her tremulous mouth. Some faint stirrings of he knew not what were in his breast.

"How sad," he said, "That the General should die when he had someone like you as his wife."

Frau von Kaisering's face lit up with satisfaction but she only said, "The Fatherland was his wedded wife."

Words. The formal words came from their lips but meant nothing. They were moving closer and closer, lust radiating like the glow from the candles in an enveloping pool. The sound of gunfire came even closer and a stray bullet whistled through one of the high windows of the crypt and richochetted around them. The widow dived to the floor on one side of the coffin while Paul threw himself down on the other.

In the midst of the battle, Helga von Kaisering found time to remove her coat: "Don't be afraid," Paul whispered. "Don't be afraid ... I'm still here." Her lilac crepe dress clung to her body like Venus' drapes, her legs were in gleaming grey silk stockings.

On the other side of the coffin she smiled to herself and said softly, "We mustn't make a sound."

"You are so brave, Frau von Kaisering ..."

"Call me Helga ... Paul .. Oh, I feel so alone, now. Oh Paul! Will you help me through this?"

Her call for help, her husky voice, the pathos of it all, the sweetness of her words all called out to Paul. He moved to her.

"Will you, Paul? Will you help and comfort me?" she asked, knowing now he was practically hers.

Memories of earlier times came to him. A stirring in his body, a response which he had once known but had never dared recognise. A reaction in his breast that matched a mood of that long forgotten time. Picture postcards and the night and words and dormitory tales of sinful adventures. He moved closer to her and she pulled him tight. Their legs entwined.

His body changed. He felt it changing and growing and it puzzled him until all the memories fell into place and Cilly and Eva made sense and an incredible, boastful smile lit his face: "I remember this," he shouted. "Victory! Victory! Victory!"

Helga von Kaisering knew what he was talking about for the victory was hers. "Then charge, Lieutenant," she ordered. "Mount and charge! Into the attack, my Lieutenant."

They grappled through the lilies, through the folds of the colours of the Fatherland, through the lilac widow's crepe, but he reached his objective. In the tight little space before the altar, there was really no room for violent movement and the back of Paul's head bounced against the General in his box, but he was oblivious to all else save the knowledge of his reawakening and his pleasure in the widow's power.

"I can do it," he said hoarsely. "I remember it now. It's called . . ."

"Yes, yes," she said, impatient for the act and not the word.

"Yes, you can do it. Do it! Do it!"

"I'm doing it," he said, not to her but to himself and he could not remember quite whether he had done it before or whether he had only heard about it and imagined how it would be. Then he thought he could never have actually done it for nothing so strong, so pleasurable as this could ever be forgotten; nothing could ever drive this pleasure away. And it was a noisy pleasure. He could hear the great guns booming in the distance and the sound of a heavy wind blowing up from deep in the valleys. "The guns!" he shouted.

"Yes? Yes?"

"The guns!" and his body moved with violence. "The great, great guns . . . in rows . . . the great, great steel barrels sticking out towards the sky . . ."

"Yes! Yes!"

"And shooting . . . Aagh . . . shooting flames . . . the great wind . . . Aagh . . ."

"Ohhh . . yes, yes!"

"The pounding, pounding . . . pounding . . .!"

"Pound! Pound!"

"The shells . . . going up the barrel . . . skywards . . . up, up, up! Exploding! I'm a gun! I'm a barrel! I'm a shell! My God! I'm exploding!"

But this time there was no answer from the widow underneath for he had set off a landmine of an explosion in her body, and where all his burning shells fell, the fertile earth was already in a turmoil.

They crept, sated, from their hiding place to find that night was near. Paul, with one empty space in his mind filled with his new knowledge, had eyes for nothing except his Frau and did not see in the distance, all alone and sad, a figure sitting upright and motionless, forgotten in the gun fire; the shell of a German colonel in a wheel chair.

Helga von Kaisering's villa was set like a jewel on a lake. It was large and beautiful and elegant, but Paul did not notice it at first.

At first he spent his time in recapturing again and again and again the barrage in the crypt, except now the set battle pieces, the charges, the lances, the shooting, the huge barrel raised with its terrible shells, took place in comfort – in Helga's bed or bath, or before dinner in front of the fire on the bear-skin rug in the drawing room, or after dinner in front of the fire on the tiger-skin rug in the dining-room when, gorged with food and wine, they had fallen from their places at table, to gnaw on each other like lions after a marrow-filled bone.

It had taken place in the freezing, snow-decked park around the house, and Helga had looked like an ice-princess, naked in mink, and he had looked her double, naked in a wolf-skin coat that brushed the snow as he walked. It had taken place in the library amid an ocean of leather-bound books on wars lost and wars won – but *they* won every battle, every time.

It had, at first, always been the same as the first time, except his head was not bruised and the General not disturbed in his resting place. Every time he had charged he had felt at one with the guns and every release was a freedom he knew he *must* enjoy many times every day.

And then, suddenly, it was not enough for Helga. He had not realised that there could be more, or that more should ever be needed.

She wanted him to relax. She wanted him to be her masculine alter ego; she wanted him to be her, had she been a prince and not a princess. She wanted him to wear white suits and walk differently; he was no longer a soldier, he was a lover, she said. She wanted him to be in the house, even when she was not there, and she locked the doors to keep him there.

He did not notice. He sat in a chair and forgot all else. He forgot his mother, Cilly, Eva, the Captain. He forgot his mission and he forgot the Kaiser. He sat in a chair in the house by the lake and waited for the bugle call which gave him an escape from the wavering past into the rock-firm present.

Then, even as caviar will pall if over-indulged in, so he longed for the urgent sound of bedroom gunfire to die down a little. Paul needed more time to think of other things and he needed other places in which to think of them.

It was then that the locked doors began to disturb him. He was always it seemed to him then, in the same room and the only exit was to the balcony high above the lake.

"Helga, why do you lock the doors?" he asked.

"Why Paul – to keep you safe, of course." She did not notice the look of almost apathetic despair on his face. "Oh Paul, you look lovely in that suit. So white, so sensuous Mmm." she said.

"I feel like a puppet," he said.

"Oh no! You're a born model ... so good to look at . move for me, while I look at you."

"Helga – I'm *here*! Isn't that enough? I don't understand any of this except I know I hate it."

"Nonsense! Now walk across the room!"

There was nothing else he could do except parade before

the suits of armour, the baronial shields of the forgotten General's family. Her voice held a tone of command learned from her husband that rang a bell in Paul from long ago. He got up and strode around her chair.

"No, darling," she said. "*Prowl.* Like a panther. Let your shoulders go slack."

Her orders only made him tighten up the more. His only knowledge of movement had been gained on the parade ground.

"No, no – flop a little!" He flopped one shoulder. "Now put a hand over your stomach as if you had a pain – and for goodness sake, smile!"

"How can I smile if I have a stomach ache?"

"Darling, darling Paul! How can I present you to my friends, make you presentable for the public, if you walk like a soldier on parade and never smile?"

"I don't want to be *presented* in public," he said, sulky.

"Maybe," she said, not listening to him, "Maybe some music would help . . ." she went to the gramophone: its horn reminded him suddenly, poignantly, of the furtive days in the U Bahn.

She wound it up and put on a record. After a few scratchy seconds, a throbbing tango filled the room. At once Helga's body throbbed with the music.

She was wearing a clinging, backless gown, high necked at the front, but showing the cleft in her lovely buttocks. The sleeves were long and flowing. It reminded Paul of a lozenge: pale pink in front and dark pink at the back. She had nothing on beneath and as she moved, the outline of her perfect, tip-tilted breasts, with sharply pointed nipples could be seen. Her belly was rounded, and the dress clung and fell over her prominent mound and on over her long, swelling thighs.

Paul felt nothing stir. He could not associate with her, or with the music. He began to move towards the door, away from her, away from the room which had kept him a willing prisoner for so long.

Helga seemed to be carried away by the music, and was dancing by herself, imagining that every sensuous quiver, every shake of breast or buttock would arouse Paul. Her body kept perfect pace with the tango, and the tango and the white suit seemed to go together in Paul's mind as symbols of sudden over-voluptuous femininity, of fecundity and the musk of sex.

Suddenly he wanted a slender nymph; a downy, blond cadet who didn't want sex at all. He wanted purity again.

Helga danced on with her eyes closed. "Paul, Paul," she called softly, sexily, huskily. "Come and dance with me!"

She arched her breasts against the light from the window and the nipples were harder, more prominent. She swung her hips in demanding suggestion, and the mound beneath the clinging silk jersey was no longer that of Venus, but that of a fertile Pacific island goddess: fat-bottomed, fat-bellied and rapacious.

He had reached the door and had one hand on the handle; it was not locked. She opened her eyes at the long silence, and saw him. Immediately she stiffened and took on the stance of an arrogant *junker*, whose lands stretched across Prussia for ever, and whose servants fawned. Paul watched the transformation fascinated:

"Come here!" she ordered. "Lieutenant – come here!"

He did not move towards her but his hand tightened on the door handle.

"It's a little late to be giving me orders, isn't it, Frau von Kaisering?"

Her body seemed to slump slightly. The arrogant stance gave way to a begging posture. "We could learn to dance the tango together." The hint of a plead.

"I think not." Cool arrogance. Withdrawal. Scorn.

She moved as if slapped, then straightened in a rage. Had she been near she might have hit him, but instead she snatched the offending record from the turntable and smashed it against her thigh. It cracked; an echo of recent gunfire; and the pieces, impotent, fell on the floor.

"I see." She spat the words at him, and waited for him to grovel, to be humble.

"Look at me! Look at me when I talk to you!" she screamed at him, at last.

Paul looked at her and saw the tears of anger on her cheeks. He was not interested, not moved, and she could see that he was not.

"Get out! Get out, Lieutenant!" she screamed.

"Thank you," he said quietly, and left the room, and immediately, the house.

* * * * *

TEN

The memory of Helga and the house by the lake faded into a weaker version of the white clouds of the Front. There was no time and no objective. Somehow he ate and somewhere he slept and nothing held him to any place or person and no desire drove him on nor any distaste held him back. It was not the freedom he had thought about when he had sat in the locked room and the locked house, but neither was it a public prison where his performance was all and the performance of the great barrel most of all. His cell, now, was bounded only by the walls of his own movements.

Movements. Trains with steam like white clouds and grey clouds with white snow or blue skies with white clouds. It was the same and a season came and went without his interest or his care.

Kraft was looking for him and so too was tired, yearning Frau von Kaisering, but all she could say to Kraft when he came, stiff and formal, was that she would rather like to find him, too. Perhaps the Captain could tell her when he found Paul?

Ladies of a certain age and fortune, who had seen him with Helga, and who had stood jealously on the sidelines, knowing she had the advantage over them of youth, beauty and fortune, mourned his passing and blamed her for having presumed too much on his person: "She was too old," they said. "Old enough to be his mother," which may have been the truth, although she was not as old, in fact, as his mother, and would have been a child-bride had she borne him.

He was oblivious to all this, and may have been trying to find the roots of childhood in the house in the country, whose long-dead animals in portrait once had littered the apartment in town, but the house in the country was long dead, too, and his roots with it.

Neither time nor thought disturbed him. He was a frog who hibernated even as he walked along the crowded village streets, and there was no kiss to metamorphose him.

Then he was back in Berlin, and the long hibernation was over. Time had made him the prince again, but without the kiss from the princess who did not exist for him, his soul was still that of the frog.

His memory was two years old but in Berlin little had changed: only the rich were richer, and fatter, and sleeker, and more desperate; and the degenerate more degenerate. And not only were the worms right out of the woodwork, but they were dancing on the top of the piano to a tune wilder than ever the Kaiser had composed. The pace was faster and more frantic; but the movements were on a carousel and the faster it went, the quicker it arrived back at the same place.

Paul went to the Turkish baths where Mutti had once worked. One part of him hoped she would not still be there, for he hated the idea; but the other part hoped that she would be, for if she were not, then it meant that Major von Meuller would be her keeper.

She was there, as always, cleaning the place for an evening clientele.

"Mutti," he said.

"Paul!"

"Hello, Mutti."

"Paul. Where have you been for such a long time?"

"Been? . . . I'm not sure . . ."

"But how are you? Have you been taking care of yourself?"

"I expect I have. At least, I feel the same as ever."

"But you keep running away and we never know where you are. What is it? What's wrong?"

Paul did not know what was wrong, or even, if anything were wrong. "I suppose something's missing . . . it all seems pretty meaningless . . ." he groped for the right words, the right way to say it so that he would understand himself, and she would understand him. ". . . the way I was taught . . . something . . ."

He gave up before he had began. "I don't know. Anyway, where's Cilly?"

The baths, marble slab upon marble slab, steaming water, were behind them. With all that space, he and his mother stood in the unhappy, yellow-tiled, peeling-ceilinged lavatory.

"Cilly? You don't know? ... no, of course not ... She's working at the Lützower Club."

Paul stood silently for a moment, trying to think of something more to say that would make his mother look less tired, less aged, more pleased to see him. There was nothing. He turned and left.

Mutti watched him go, then went back to polishing the yellow tiles.

In broad daylight, the Lützower Club lost some of its glamour but for all that, its pseudo elegance made Paul aware that his clothes looked less than smart. He hestitated for several minutes before ringing the bell. Then he stood back and waited.

A fat woman opened the door and he asked if Cilly were there:

"A friend of hers, are you?" she asked and she let him in before he had time to answer.

Inside the club, all the lights were on full and daylight came through the uncurtained windows. At night Paul could imagine that the place would look dark and sophisticated, but right now its tattiness was revealed.

Cilly was sitting on a table rehearsing one of her numbers. She had sung it for him once before, only now, she didn't know that he was there, and it sounded strangely forlorn to him.

"*... Young ladies who plan and scheme to get rich ... will become poor old maids only married to money ...*" She swung her legs, crossing them; flash of white thigh, stockings as high as her crotch, breasts tumbling out of wired cups ... "*I need no rich man's plenty ... they're always seventy ... a Lieutenant around twenty ...*" She lifted her head tossing her mane of golden curls. In that instant she saw Paul and her face froze. "*... is good enough ... is good enough ...* her voice faltered. She rallied. "*Is good enough to fall in love with me!*" she sang firmly and gaily.

Then she was off the table, running in her high heels to Paul.

"Well darling," lisped the pansy choreographer to her back, "I think once more from the top, don't you?"

She and Paul looked at each other, and it was as if each had discovered something that had not been there before.

"I'm no longer twenty," Paul said simply.

Now they were wandering through the Tiergarten again, just as they had before. Specifically, they were walking by a huge statue: "That's you," she said laughing. "My monument without the pigeon shit! . . . Oh, it's lovely to have you back, Lieutenant."

"Thanks – but don't call me that," he said.

"Why not?"

"I don't know . . . it's just that it's started to bother me recently . . . Anyway, enough of that. Aren't you going to ask me where I've been . . . how I've been?"

"There's no need for that," she said. "I can tell that just by looking at you."

"So, how *have* I been?" he asked.

"Suffering!" She sighed dramatically. "Suffering but complacent. And suicidal like a wildebeest near a pride of lions. But you can forget all that now . . . forget and be happy. And you can tell everybody you knew me way back when."

"Way back when what?"

"Before I was famous! – Oh, of course, you don't know, do you? I'm famous now!"

"And what happened to politics and the great revolution . . . weren't you supposed to be a child of the revolution . . . ?" He was surprised that finally, he was able to tease, to feel relaxed – almost to feel happy.

"It took too long in coming," she said. "So I switched my ambitions and became a great cabaret lady, darling!"

"Switching seems to be one of my problems, too," he said.

"What a lot of problems you have, darling!" she said, and kissed him. "Tell me – is shell shock and '*you know what*' still one of them?"

She kissed Paul again, lightly, on the mouth and he pulled her tightly to him. The reaction in his body was so fast, so instantaneous, he thought he might burst. Up and down the length of them was the answer to her cryptically-asked question. He moved against her in a grinding hold.

"What do you think?" he asked when the long kiss was over.

She broke away from him and ran across the grass, laughing.

"I don't think you still have *that* problem," she shouted back over her shoulder, "... but I haven't time to make absolutely certain now. Come to the club this evening and we'll go into it deeper . . ."

The club at night, was suddenly glamorous, even when he looked closely. The stains on the carpet could not be seen in the dull light and the clean linen and sparkling crystal on the tables made a big difference. Most of all, though, thought Paul, it was the customers who made the place seem chic.

Some strange customers; men made up like women and some even with dresses on; some women in severely tailored British-styled suits and cropped hair. Straightforward elegance from the aristocracy of the business world, though the women were probably no better than high-class whores; and pansies who were interested in real men and not those who were pretending to be women; theatre people; people who were there to see and people who were out to be seen.

The lights went out and a grotesque transvestite took the spotlight: "Ladies and gentlemen!" The words came, half soprano and half bass from the mouth which was one bright splodge of vermillion lip rouge.

"Ladies and gentlemen . . . the moment you have all been waiting for: the wickedest girl in Germany . . . LYA TABOO!!"

Paul was startled for a moment when Cilly walked on the stage and began to sing. Then he realised that she was Lya Taboo and that to judge from the interest the audience were showing, she was indeed famous.

She was dressed like a well brought up vamp with more knowledge of perversion than was good for her. Black sequins were on a figure-hugging net that left nothing to the imagination and she moved like a seal. Her body was entirely covered with gold dust that caught the shaded lights so that even her skin glowed and she used blue and green peacocks' feathers as if she were Cleopatra about to seduce every Anthony in Berlin.

Paul marvelled slightly that this slim, small figure could hold the room the way she did, then she looked directly at him, and he saw that her eyes were brilliant aquamarine and so hypnotic that he felt drawn to her; he had never noticed her eyes before as being so special.

Her song was sad; she was waiting for a man to come along, someone she had bought a new dress and perfume for, but the bar was closing even though a tune was still playing ... "*Why is it, it's always me; left here by myself you see ... A little tired of waiting with the chairs upturned ... feeling spurned ...*"

It was a sad song and it made Paul feel sad. "*... My hopes, my schemes, seem only dreams ... He will not come today ...*

In the dim glow as the carpet looked clean so did Paul. Clean and handsome and very interesting. He interested a man sitting nearby, a good-looking man wearing evening dress; but other people had eyes only for Cilly.

At the next table three people sat, and two of them were glued to the little stage and "Lya Taboo", while a third man was as intently studying them. He was a fat man and dressed like a German equivalent to a Broadway agent. The other two, thought Paul, were certainly the real thing – Americans from America.

One, entirely in white, with a long white silk scarf, had the air of authority which told all interested that he was the boss. His actions were authoritarian, he was aggressive in his movements, his voice was powerful and he knew what was good and what was bad.

"She's sparkling," he said when Cilly had finished her number.

The other American looked like an expensive clown. His clothes were an outrageous mixture of dazzling colours: "She's wonderful," he stated.

"I said 'sparkling', Lynne. Sppar-kk-linG!!"

"Yes, sir," he said, a crestfallen cockatoo.

The fat German had followed this brief sally and had now translated the meaning into his own language for his own benefit. "You think so?" he asked.

The two Americans answered in unison much to the irritation of the man in white. "Absolutely!" Then, as if to show who was the boss, the boss man said, "Naturally, that hat will have to go."

The German was agitated: "Hat?" he queried.

"Yes! . . . we'll dye her hair pink."

"Sparkling pink," said the buffoon and sat back to await approval. He got a look of intense hatred for his pains.

The German was nonplussed. "Gentlemen . . . I am her agent . . . of course, but I don't believe . . ."

"And her teeth! – How are her teeth?"

"Her teeth?" the agent was startled.

"Sure – her teeth. You've no idea, but it's become one of our biggest problems with these European imports. Something to do with the diet or the calcium level of the water, or something."

The German agent fought back. "But we have the highest calcium content in Europe," he protested, as if it really were true.

"We get a lot of problems with teeth," said the multi-coloured lover.

"Gentlemen . . . Gentlement . . . She's a singer, not a racehorse, or a trapeze artiste who swings by her teeth . . . I mean . . ."

The man in white cut across these protestations. "And how about sentimental attachments? Any of those, eh? Any young Hans in lederhosen hanging around? Any potential scandal?"

"We have problems with scandal too," said the boyfriend.

Paul was interested to hear the agent's answer; it seemed to him that anyone who looked like "Lya Taboo" must have a life as full of scandal at least as all the bizarre clientele of the club who were there to watch her.

"Cilly's only interested in her work. There's no man in her life, and no scandal."

Paul wondered why he felt relieved to hear the words – since he knew that whatever the truth, the agent would have returned the same answer.

"Well, anyway, she was great," said the man in white.

"We gotta talk to her an' fix things up."

The agent, who had been growing more depressed by the minute during this interchange about teeth and scandal took a little time to digest this. "You mean – you want to talk to her?" he said somewhat startled.

"Sure I do," said the boss. "She'll be the greatest thing to hit Hollywood since . . ."

"Rin Tin Tin!" supplied the rainbow.

"Al Jolson!" glowered the man in his life.

* * * * *

ELEVEN

Paul waited nervously outside the Lützower. He was aware of how shabby he looked. Inside, there were men offering Cilly a new, rich, fabulous life in Hollywood. Fame and fortune in exchange for her signature on a contract. He doubted she would join him now.

Suddenly the door opened and she pranced out still wearing the costume from her last number. "Sorry," she said breathlessly, "I've been talking to some Americans. I didn't want to keep you waiting so I came as I am." She was dressed in white, practically naked. But she dragged a huge white fur boa. She had white ribbons in her hair, and wore white silk gloves. She looked as if she were about to be the bride at a pornographic wedding party.

Paul waved at a huge limousine taxi parked a little way up the street. "I heard them talking, the Americans," he said. "I suppose you're going to Hollywood now?"

"I haven't made up my mind ... yet. Anyway, if I go, it certainly won't be tonight!" She giggled. "I have other plans!"

The taxi drew up and she opened the door. "Get in," she said and slipped in beside him.

"To the Swanenwerder," she ordered.

"But that's miles away!" Paul said.

"You'll love it when you get there," she said. "And ... you'll like the drive ..." she smiled, wickedly. "Now, how did you like the show?"

"I wasn't sure what I expected ... I mean, the place ... the people ... all that. Still, I expect you can cope you seem so much more adaptable than me."

"Yes, I expect you're right," she murmured vaguely, snuggling up close to him so that the huge boa swamped him and he could feel her silk-clad legs and smell her scent.

"I don't know what it is," he said, feeling that suddenly Cilly had grown up and overtaken him and was no longer the girl with the scar from skating who looked for a cadet on a white charger ... "... but I don't seem to have any way of measuring life any more ... no yardstick to set against the future ... Everything's by ear, from day to day, moment to moment. Life floats, and there's no sheet anchor. Floating ... you know?"

"Or soaring like a bird without a nest to build, or young to feed ... Soaring out into the blue sky ... Free and footloose," she suggested pointedly.

"Rather dramatic!"

"That's how I feel ... don't you?"

"Me? said Paul. "Me? I feel useless."

Outside the window of the comfortable car the city's lights floated by in a haze of falling snow. Inside the cab it was warm and Paul felt the excitement and affection and lust rise through his body. It was a nice feeling. He wondered if it might be a true lover's feeling the feeling of a true lover and not of a man who was about to simply sleep with a woman. He had never been in love. He wouldn't know how to recognise it, he realised.

The taxi crossed a wide bridge and entered the ultra smart residential area of Swanenwerder. Sat far back from the road, behind walls and high, old trees, he could see the twinkling lights from the unshuttered windows of the big town houses. He wondered who Cilly knew out there, or whether she was so famous that she actually owned her own villa now.

The taxi swung off the road at her command and went up a curving drive towards a high, magnificent mansion. The car stopped at the base of a wide, statue-lined flight of stone steps and Cilly got out, looking up towards the doors of the house. Although she had practically nothing on, and the snow was now quite heavy, she glowed. Paul managed to keep his eyes off her and pay the driver, then Cilly caught him by the arm and went skipping up the steps like a circus pony.

"Isn't it lovely!" she said as she opened the door with a key. "It's got everything! Seventy rooms ... and dogs ... cats ... servants ... silver ... ! Come on, in here!" and she led him into the drawing room, and Paul, impressed by its size, stared about him, taking in the rich and rare furniture, the gilt, the crystal, the marble, the *objets*, while she was throwing cushion after cushion into a heap before the dying fire. That done, she piled fresh logs on, and poked it into a crackling blaze.

"We'll make the bed here," she said.

"Bed?" he said. "Suppose someone comes in?"

"They won't – there's no one here tonight, but us," she said calmly. "The Prince said so."

"The Prince?"

"Yes – he comes with the house ... and I can have the house, too ... as soon as I say I'll marry him!" she said casually. "Come on!" She pulled him down beside her on the great mound of silken and velvet cushions.

"What are you doing now?" he asked.

"Taking my clothes off, of course," It seemed to him she was already practically naked. "I have found it much easier making love with my clothes off. Here, let me help you ..." she said and began unfastening his buttons.

Half memories of strict, almost Lutheran sermons floated back. Purity and sanctity interlaced and interlarded with schoolboy sniggering and a feeling for what was right. It was as if the interlude with Helga had never been.

"Of course, doing this with a whore ... but I wouldn't like to think the girl I was going to marry ..." He pushed her hands away. "*What are you doing?*" he asked desperately.

"Giving you a helping hand," she said, and proceeded to do so. He gasped at the exquisite shock – but it was such a shock that he wilted before her subtle onslaught.

"Oh do come on," she cajoled. "I've been waiting for you for three years – more if you count for ever! Let's not waste any more time now."

"Where's your sense of decency? Somebody might come in!"

"They won't!"

"It's not right!" A last protesting cry for now he was frightened that his sudden flush of high morals might be misinterpreted as impotence. With Cilly, to date, he had put up no show at all.

She sat up and looked at him in the firelight. Her teeth and the string of pearls about her neck glowed with the same, equal lustre. He thought the clowns from Hollywood should see her now.

"Paul, do you love me ... or don't you?"

"That's not the point!" Her body was lovely ... he felt a throb ... the guns were elevating.

"What is the point, then?"

"We should wait until the Kaiser comes back," he said inanely. "Wait until there's a time of decency, when people can bring up a family ..."

"Are you mad?" she said, amazed. "What family? Where have you been all your life? I want to make love, not start a baby!" She eyed him very strangely.

"But – this is how you get babies," he protested, stung. "Don't you know that? This just isn't the time ... sex should mean marriage and security ..."

"Balls!" she said. "Security went out of the window long ago ... or didn't you know that, my sleeping beauty ...?" Her knowledgeable hands stole over his body once more and the great guns were ready again, once more lifting to the sky. His mind grew hazy in the delicious sensations and he couldn't understand why he was protesting; he couldn't even remember his motive for refusing.

"Paul, Paul," she whispered and her hand was inside his shirt.

"We don't have much time ..." she said.

He began to respond, but gently and without vigour. She climbed on top of him and kissed him over and over. He felt the heat from the fire and her body, but just as his excitement began to reach the peak where he was ready for her, he suddenly felt exposed in that huge, luxurious room, with its two pairs of double doors, and the fireplace big enough to conceal a regiment up its gaping chimney.

"It's too hot down here," he said slipping from beneath her.

"Then let's go up to the bedroom – I don't mind, just as long as you're happy. I need you now."

He didn't know if he were happy or not. He knew he wanted her urgently and that his balance had gone again. He suddenly tried to recall if this was the same feeling he had with Helga. It wasn't. It wasn't better, or worse – but it was different. It almost certainly wasn't true love.

In the bedroom she tried to undress him again, but his hands were surer and faster. "Have you much experience?"

he asked her, remembering that once, long ago, he had wondered if she had a lover.

"Nothing that won't put you to shame," she said and lay on the vast bed and watched him undress. He had been faintly scandalised that she had strolled up the curving staircase totally naked. "Mmm, that's better," she said. "You seem to be ready for me . . ."

"I am." He didn't want to do this in the light; he was shy.

"Put out the light, Cilly."

He felt the luxurious rush and then he was home and safe and able to relax and feel the great peace which comes before the battle. The birds singing at dawn, just before the artillery opens fire at the onset of another great and bloody attack, which leads to nowhere but the grave and the white clouds.

"Cilly! Cilly!"

Her voice, soft and gurgling, "Ohhh! Ohhhh . . . OHHH!!" came close and strangely into his left ear when all along he had imagined she was a million miles beneath him as he plunged down on the one hand, and where he floated high up on the other, and joined only by the most tenuous and delightful link with earth and the girl.

"Cilly! I can't hold on . . . they'll blow the whistle and over the top."

"Blow," she screamed . . . "Blow the walls down!"

It was very different. After Helga there had been a madness; a desire to fight the whole battle again immediately. To charge in, cost what it might and only the pure physical exhaustion finally stopped him and it never stopped Helga. Now, with Cilly, that mood was replaced by a strange feeling of deep contentment. The act itself was no less exhilarating, but the after effects were so different:

"With Helga, I ate but was still hungry," he said to himself, "But with this girl, the feast has satisfied."

He had only just finished the thought before sleep; deep and unmarked by any dreams. As the sun threw out the first, false dawn over the house, reflecting from the thick layer of snow, Paul slipped quietly away to a land where, except for amnesia, he had not been for a very long time.

Cilly was not quite the same person after, but she was

more practical about it. Her desire for Paul had been the desire a girl has for her first love, but unfortunately both for Paul and herself, time had passed between the time of desire and the time of fulfilment and others had taken her first.

Other lovers in fact and other lovers in fiction. She was too world weary, now for Paul, though at that moment neither of them quite recognised it. What she hadn't experienced, others had talked about to her so that her thoughts were different. She had wanted Paul both romantically and physically – but she had been curious, too; and now that the curiosity had been satisfied, she found herself a little restless and wondering whether the wait had been worthwhile. In fact, he made love like any other man with whom she was not in love and that, rather alarmingly for her romantic dreams, told her that she was *not* in love with him; and it also told her why she had not got what she had expected. In the end she decided that it had been worthwhile but her false dawn brought no false hope.

She woke while he was still deep in sleep. She felt fine and happy and glad – and, yes, satisfied. She could have felt let down and was glad that she did not.

She found a robe and went downstairs. In the hall, her agent was waiting, let in by she knew not whom, although it was still very early. In the shadows, unseen by either, sat the Prince.

"Cilly! Cilly!" the fat man cried in relief.

"Max! Whatever are you doing here at this time of the morning?" she said crossly.

"Cilly, you'll catch cold dressed like that," he said, ignoring both the tone and the question.

"– Oh, Max! What is it? What do you want can't I ever get any peace?"

"It's the Americans . . . they've made an offer . . . Enough to fill the whole house with dollars!"

"Does this place look as if it needs it?" she said, not believing him.

"No – but you do – and so do I . . . They want to see you right away . . .!" He was out of breath with the urgency of his message.

"What now?" She wanted to go back upstairs to make

love again with Paul, to explore it again, to see if it were any better or worse, without the excitement of it being *the first time*, finally, with him.

"Right now . . . Hollywood beckons, my songbird!"

She stared at him, her eyes widening at the magic word. "Give me a minute," she said, and went back up the stairs to bathe.

Paul was still asleep, but there was no need to disturb him – last night's garments were still scattered about the drawing room, but the Prince had filled a dressing-room for her, where she dressed quickly, and without a backward glance for Prince or new lover, she ran out into the snow and down the flight of stairs to the taxi where Max was waiting.

"HOLLYWOOD!" she cried to the driver.

The taxi drew away and seemed to float through the mist now rising from the lake and all the trees had icicles. The Prince stepped out from the darkened doorway into the chill snow, and stared after the taxi with brooding eyes. He was still in full evening dress.

Paul awoke a long time after his lady had flown. He awoke with fine feelings and wished she were alongside him to take advantage of his warmth. But there was no hurry.

He found the adjoining white and blue Wedgewood bathroom and drew a hot bath and got in to soak. He lay in the water full length so that just his face appeared above the surface. The bath was a solid slab of pale grey marble, and the soap was pleasant and creamy.

He heard the door open and spoke without moving. "Cilly . . . good morning . . ."

He froze when the voice that answered behind him was deep and manly: "Good morning. Did you sleep well?"

Paul sat up in the bath and tried to smile at the tall, powerfully-built man. "Yes," he said. "Yes, fine, thank you."

"And is there plenty of hot water?"

"Oh yes. Lovely . . . very hot . . ." He felt at a decided disadvantage . . . was this a valet? He seemed very sure of himself.

To cover his confusion, and to show that he felt at ease, he started to wash himself again, but his fear was such that he squeezed the soap too hard and it shot from his hands and landed at the man's feet. Very casually, the tall man speared the block with his cane and handed it back to Paul, then he sat down, relaxed, assured, by the side of the tub.

"You must be the Prince," said Paul.

"Yes. Yes, I am."

"This is a wonderful house," Paul ventured.

The Prince smiled wanly. "We like it," he said.

"Um ... (what the hell?) ... have you been a Prince long (Oh, Lord) ... I mean ..."

"All my life and all my family's life for many generations back."

"King's ... (don't be so ludicrous) ... kings in the family, ever?"

The Prince smiled, but the smile made Paul tense. "Five," he said. "Five kings in all," he smiled again. "Two of whom were murdered by their brothers."

"Ohmm ... Er, really? ... any particular reason for that?"

"Yes. They would insist on sleeping with other people's mistresses."

Paul felt the unease grow, but more especially, he felt foolish. Words were hard to think of and conversation of any value impossible.

"I think I'm clean now," he said brightly.

The Prince did not take the hint. Paul looked down at himself; things looked different when seen through water, and some things looked more ridiculous than they had any right to. He looked up. The towel horse was across the width of the bathroom away. He glanced sideways at the Prince and at once met his very bright blue eyes. Blue eyes locked with blue eyes for a split second, and Paul felt the hair rising on the nape of his neck.

"I wonder if you would be very kind, and pass me a towel? Once I'm dried, I'll be up and on my way."

"Of course," said the Prince. "No hurry, though," and he stretched out his cane again without moving and hoisted a towel off the rail and passed it to Paul.

Paul jiggled himself up, trying to keep both his back and his front concealed from the Prince and all the time using the towel to cover his nakedness without actually dropping the ends in the water. He tried a weak smile during these contortions, and the Prince smiled back. "You know Prince ... I've known Cilly an awful long time ... Ever since we were ..."

The Prince saved him further, ludicrous explanation by reaching out and putting his hand about three feet from the tiled floor. "About since you were so high?" he suggested.

"Yes ... that's right; since we were both about so high." As if that made the fact of the previous night's abandonment any better ... He was standing up completely now, and the skimpy towel – he noted there were other, huge ones – was hugging closely round his hips.

"I'm sure you've known her ... since you shared a ... cot ..." said the Prince. "But, of course, you're not ..." and he spread his hand again, "... that high, any more, are you ...?"

The Prince stood up and Paul, with the added advantage of the bath beneath his feet, was still only a little taller and sadly a great deal less powerful.

"I'm sorry about this," he stuttered. "I really didn't know anything ... I mean ..."

The Prince opened the bathroom door. "We'll talk about it when you're dressed," he said and went out of the room.

Paul was in a state approaching something like panic – and where was Cilly? The Prince had given him no clue at all.

When he was dressed and feeling a little less vulnerable, Paul went down stairs. The Prince was waiting and led him through the drawing room and out onto the terrace. In the snowy morning light, Paul could see now just how imposing the pile of masonry was.

"You see all this?" asked the Prince, waving a careless hand forward to take in the glistening park, and backwards to indicate the house. "You'd think it would be enough to attract any woman, wouldn't you?"

Paul nodded and gulped silently. The Prince's voice was even and without passion but maybe he didn't require a spate of noise and ranting to build up to murder.

"Well, my boy, it's not enough and I tell you, it never is. They always want that little something extra ... like *you* ...

for example." He turned and looked almost fondly at Paul and Paul had the sudden chill feeling that the Prince did, indeed know him most intimately . . . but the lights had been off . . . the room had been dark. What about earlier downstairs before that massive fireplace . . . ? Could he – had he . . . ?

"In the end," continued the Prince, you find it's quite natural, and you grow to accept it – their always wanting just that little bit more than is offered . . . ?" He sighed almost nostalgically for the women who once, had eagerly taken what was given them, with grateful hands and grateful hearts. "We Princes have to get used to the situation . . . become just that little more sophisticated than the average man in the street. In the old days we killed the cuckold in the nest – these days . . . well, there it is." The Prince laid a hand on Paul's shoulder and Paul jumped as if he had been shot. "I shouldn't worry about it if I were you."

While Paul was wondering just exactly what it was he shouldn't be worrying about, it occurred to him that he still hadn't seen Cilly. He imagined that the Prince might think it tacky of him to raise the subject, thereby causing grief, pain or even injury. However, he also felt it would look somewhat gauche to leave the Prince's house without even enquiring of the whereabouts, and perhaps, good health, of the young lady who had brought him here.

"I say, Prince," he said, and it came out oddly anyway. "I say – is Cilly around?"

"Back to town," came the disinterested answer.

"Back to town? Already?"

"A fat man, called Max, I believe, came for her in a taxi," said the Prince, bored. "He's her agent, I imagine." Paul remembered, from the night before in the Lützower. "He came, very excitedly, shouting about money. Perfectly vulgar. But very strange, for it excited her too. I think the truth is the fame, not the money. After all, I could give her – money." The Prince vaguely waved about him. "But you can't fight the urge for fame, you know."

"Or glory."

"Or glory," said the Prince.

* * * * *

TWELVE

The swans were fighting on the lake. He walked down the long curve of the drive in the centre of the parallel marks made by the taxi that had come for Cilly and taken her away. Was she really going to Hollywood...? It seemed impossible.

His Cilly was a revolutionary – a singer of the people, and he had had that image of her so long that even her success in the Lützower seemed as unreal as last night's love affair; as insubstantial as the mist that was swirling rapidly about him as he walked.

When would things ever be real again? He had walked through mist and dreams and nightmares until they were more real than reality. What was reality ... was it simply a feeling of safety and security ... or was it a feeling that he was not sleep-walking his days away...?

The mist suddenly lifted and whirled back towards the house, obliterating it; and, then, last night, and the Prince, and the bath and Cilly had never existed. They faded back into the realms of magic where they belonged.

The lake sparked and the swans rose towards each other, treading water, which sparkled and rippled from their dripping black legs, and their huge wings fanned out and the sun shone through the outspread feathers of their wings which became silver and gold. Then they were screaming across the lake towards the lawns, leaving a silver wake; two sets of parallel lines, like the lines of the taxi through the snow.

It was impossible to get a taxi at Swanenwerder, where everyone had a fleet of limousines; and he had no money. No money; no work; and an old suit. Reality, when he got down to it, had a shabby ring.

Victory? Victory was his only in bed. He caught a bus back to town.

Cilly was flanked by the two Americans in the centre of their huge, hired car. Max followed in the car behind, with all the luggage. They were travelling on the Paris express, and thence to Cherbourg and the Titanic.

Cilly was lost in a sea of white mink. One American was also in white: his travelling coat was of wool, lined with mink. His companion wore red fox. The car was large, but the driver thought he would need a shoe horn to stuff them in.

"Goodness, darlings," Cilly cried with easy familiarity, "We look like a zoo!"

"Thank God for Hollywood," said the boss lover. "It's hot there."

"It'll be hotter when the little lady gets there," said the other.

"I want her cool – cool and lady-like," said the first with a scowl.

"Cool, like a Russian princess."

"She's gonna be Swedish," said the boss.

"Swedish! Great . . . yes, sir! Cool northern beauty . . ."

"Hot fires smouldering . . ." said the boss nastily. He turned to look at his lover. "Jesus, Lynne, I don't know what I see in you."

Cilly started to laugh. She laughed with her mouth wide open, and her laughter was so joyous, so infectious, that the two Americans joined in. They laughed all the way to the station.

After three years the tart was fatter than ever. On Hilda's cooking and the only exercise bed exercise, her dimples now had dimples.

Paul stopped in the door of her room, which was closed only when she had a visitor. And then, the room was always so full of the violence of her fat passion, that the door could just as easily have been left open, so public were the noises. Paul had noticed that little men: little, balding men, seemed to prefer her. Over the months, when he had lived there immediately after the war, he had seen a succession of these little men scuttling in and out like nervous piglets running for a suck at the sow's tit. It seemed stranger to him, because he had no doubt that the same men, who came to her for solace, had mountainous wives at home, and they were merely exchanging one huge dumpling for another.

She stared back at him with scarcely a flicker of interest. He could not recall that she had ever spoken to him and his blond beauty unmoved her. In Amsterdam or Munich, she would have been at a window, with all the other whores: but here, her reputation spread by word of mouth, or perhaps, he thought, there were advertisements "Mama pig seeks little paying piglets" but, still she sat in her open room as if she were at a window on the street.

"Ha! Paul! Back then!" Paul was slapped on the back. Major von Mueller smiled ferociously at him and adjusted his monocle. He had a gold-rimmed one now, Paul noted, and he looked sleeker, more dangerously sham that ever. These days he smelled of violets.

Paul smiled, a small frozen grimace that slipped away before it had time to settle.

"How's tricks ... life been treating you well?" The Major's eyes travelled rapidly over Paul's shabby suit as if assessing how long he had slept in it and how much it had cost originally. He probably, thought Paul cynically, had organised the import of the material on the black market in the first place. There was a scream from the kitchen and Mutti came running out, carrying a chopper. She stopped in mid-scream when she saw Paul. Blood dripped off the axe. "Paul . . . !"

There was a thumping noise from the kitchen. "Oh my God!" said Mutti and rolled up her eyes as she fainted.

Paul and the Major ran forward and hauled her up into a seated position, while Paul took the axe and cautiously contemplated the kitchen door. The thumping noise was more frenzied. There was a flopping sound and a slither, and his spine chilled. The Major had a wild look in his eyes and he started to drag Mutti along the passage, her two limp feet trailing lines in the carpet.

Paul suddenly had the outrageous idea that his mother had murdered his father in the kitchen or, at least, swiped at him with the axe, and the Colonel had been shocked out of his cataleptic state, and even now was slithering across the kitchen floor. The tingle in his spine spread to his fingers and toes and he was rooted.

Thump! thump! Slither, slither!

"Oh my God!" he said, and fell back into the arms of Eva, who had been drawn from her room by the screams.

"Paul!" she said. "What is it . . . what has happened?"

"Murder!" he said.

"Murder? Don't be foolish! Who is there here to murder?" She was cool, amused. "Come, let's look."

The kitchen table was a sea of blood, as was the floor, in long red streaks. His father's body was not there. But there were the various parts of a gigantic dog fish leaping in contortion over the floor.

"It wouldn't die! I hit it, and it wouldn't die," wailed Mutti from the doorway. The Major was in anxious attendance.

"What is it, what is it?" he said. His monocle was nowhere in sight.

"A fish," said Paul.

"Don't be foolish! – how could a fish . . ."

That was the second time Paul had been called a fool. He pointed at the floor. "There's your foolish fish," he said.

The four of them stared at the bloody sections, each of which had a life of its own as they humped and slithered, trailing blood at both ends. The head of the huge fish, mouth agape, eyes gleaming, suddenly seemed to leap straight up at them and they fell back into the hall, while the Major slammed the door in its teeth.

"Who'd have thought . . .!" Mutti sobbed.

"Devil fish!" exclaimed the Major.

"I think I'll lunch out today," Eva said coolly. Paul saw in amazement that she was laughing. Her lips quivered and her enchanting dimples showed as she ducked her head to conceal her amusement.

The door to Paul's old room flew open and a man, neat in blue business suit and brown brogues emerged. He stopped, alarmed at the accusing eyes which turned on him, and his face blushed scarlet.

"Do come again soon, darling," said the China Doll from behind him. "Oh . . .!" she stared down the passage.

The man attempted to beat a hasty retreat back into her room, and she pushed him forward. "Not *now*, darling," she said. He hesitated, then marched forward, attempting to disguise his face inside his brown homburg.

"Good morning Herr von Putzdorf," Mutti said as he reached them. She put out her hand to shake his, then withdrew it – it was covered in blood. "How are you keeping, then? Haven't seen you for a long time ... and your lovely wife, Frau von Putzdorf ...?"

"Well, thank you. We are both well." He spoke formally, his eyes flickering anxiously, searching for a quick escape.

"Lovely ... lovely ... Tell Frau von Putzdorf she must come to tea on Saturday. It is the anniversary of the Kaiserin's wedding."

"... Anniversary. Very well, I will tell her ... excuse me," and he made a sudden dive for the door, slamming it behind him. They heard the clatter of his departing steps.

"Such a strange man," said Mutti musingly. "I haven't seen him for such a long time, I thought he was dead ..."

"Is this a political meeting?" asked the China Doll. She had a green carnation on the ribbon round her neck. Her lashes were long and spiky, and false ones had been painted on her cheeks like spiders' legs. Her mouth was a scarlet rosebud.

"I am cooking a fish," said Mutti despairingly.

"A fish ...?"

"It won't die. It just won't die and let me cook it in peace!" Mutti said, extending her bloody hands.

The China Doll fished in her peignoir pockets for a black Russian cigarette and looked about for a light. The Major leapt forward with a gold lighter. "Thank you darling," she said, puffing smoke into his face.

She pushed the door of the kitchen open and looked at the carnage within. "Some fish!" she said, kicking the head aside with her black swansdown slipper. "It's a shark!" The head at once sprang to life with violent leaps and snaps and it careered around the kitchen table.

The China Doll stepped gingerly over the blood and guts and fish sections, which now were twitching on the floor, to the stove on which reposed a steaming pan. "I suppose you want to eat this for lunch?"

Mutti cast her eyes to heaven in affirmation.

"Well, let's see ..." said the China Doll, glancing about

her. Her eyes fell on the laundry tongs. "... Ahh!" She grasped the wooden object and swiftly scooped up a portion of fish and dropped it into the cauldron. Within moments the kitchen was cleared of leaping fish; the head was the last to go into the pot and the China Doll gave it a poke with the tongs to submerge it in the boiling stock. "There!" she said satisfied.

She turned to her aghast audience. "You must never let a dogfish beat you," she declared. "They never know when to die, those buggers ... now, where's the saffron ... and Frau von Przygodski, perhaps you'd like to clean up the blood a little, eh?"

They had lunched. Mutti and the Major had enjoyed the bouillabaise enormously and had smacked their lips and laughed over the antics of the fish who refused to die and be cooked for their pleasure.

Paul was horrified at their attitude and sulkily refused to eat. He was not hungry, he said.

"But, my darling, you will die of hunger. You are so thin, now ... don't you think he is thin?" she appealed to the Major who nodded cheerfully, his gluttony satisfied.

"Too thin. Bag of bones." He touched his napkin to his mouth.

"Damned good meal – just the thing for this weather."

"You must eat, Paul," Hilda urged. She stood up and started to ladle a serving for him.

"No – no. Really, Aunt Hilda. I had such a huge breakfast..."

"Really?" said his mother. "Where did you eat it?"

"At Swanenwerder," he said, feeling faint with hunger.

"At Swanenwerder!" exclaimed his mother, wondering who he knew there.

"At Swanenwerder!" exclaimed Hilda, who was still laughing over the account of the cooking of the fish.

"Deserve to be lined up and shot!" proclaimed the Major. "That lot at Swanenwerder – racketeers and black-marketeers, the whole collection – how else can they afford to live there?"

"Family money?" suggested Mutti.

"Family money – don't give me that!" the Major thumped the table. "No such thing today. Swept away with the Kaiser! Mark my words, things will be different when Kraft and his lot are properly organised. Germany will show them!"

"Will the Kaiser come back again?" Mutti asked.

"We'll have a glorious future," the Major said, ignoring her question. "Glorious!"

"Did you hear that, Gustav?" Hilda asked, poking some fish stew into the paralysed man's mouth, and mopping it up as it dribbled down his chin. "Did you hear that – the glory will be back . . ."

"*Deutschland uber alles*," said Paul, and got up and left the room.

He wanted, suddenly to sit with Eva. He stopped outside her door and listened. Silence. He raised his hand to knock, then let it drop.

The door opened. "Come in," Eva said.

Paul glanced at the door as he entered. He had the strange feeling that she had a one way mirror there, but the door was bare; the barest surface in the whole room.

"I wasn't sure . . . I thought you were lunching out . . ."

"Yes, I was. But then, I thought some fruit and some wine would do me more good. One eats too much stodge and not enough fresh stuff in this weather, don't you think?"

"I think you're very beautiful," he said, suddenly audacious, and surprised at his audacity. Perhaps it was because he was light-headed with hunger. It seemed weeks since he had eaten. He couldn't even remember his last meal.

"Well, you know, Paul – I think you are remarkably beautiful too," she said solemnly. He had a feeling she was laughing, but when he stared, all he could see was a faint curve to her perfect mouth and dimples. "You know – you seem to grow younger – how old are you now . . . twenty-one? twenty-two?"

"I can't remember," he said. He paused. "I really can't. I don't even know what year it is."

"It doesn't much matter," she said. "These days, that's the only real way to be."

"Timeless?"

"Ageless, too."

She poured him some wine in a pretty glass with enamelled fleurs de lys and trailing vine leaves, and she cut him some brie cheese, which she arranged with white grapes.

"Where do you get the grapes from, in this season?" he asked.

"I have a friend with hot houses . . ." she said indifferently.

Paul ate the grapes and cheese very slowly, savouring their freshness. "I was sure I was never given a decent cheese like this in France, when in hospital," he said. "I can't remember eating anything but soup."

"Can you remember France?"

"Nothing – but I can speak French. Somehow, I forgot all else, but the language."

"But you were taught French when a boy?"

"Yes. Yes, I suppose so . . . with a German accent! Now I can speak French with a peasant accent . . . very useful."

"You'd like to go to France again – I mean, to see it in a different light?"

"Yes. I would like to be a tourist – to be a rich tourist, and to do all the things that my father did before he . . ."

She nodded understandingly. "All you beautiful young men have lost your youth – that is, you are still young, of course. But you have lost what is your right, and the right of all young men. To be thoughtlessly gay and foolish when young. And now it is the old – men like your father who have abandoned care and become like children."

"And the women who have lost their youth through the war – what about them?"

She smiled faintly. "It doesn't matter about women – we always adjust to new values – we always fit in – we can always batten off men." She laughed.

"I think," Paul said slowly and carefully, "I think it must be wonderful to live without care . . . perhaps to live off women, yet to not be possessed by one."

"Like a whore, you mean, don't you?"

"Yes. Like a whore. To be paid for your body. Then to leave. To be just a gigolo, I suppose."

And then it was night again, and he was back in the little box room, and over the well was Cilly's room, the one she had had from childhood. Her unmarried mother had been the von Pryzgodski housekeeper for so long, and Cilly had been there ever since he could remember. Her mother no longer was the housekeeper to the family, but to the whole block, and now the family had no money at all, and his mother was a cleaner of sorts – just like Cilly's mother. It was a strange world.

He had made up his mind to go to the Lützower that evening to see if Cilly were there, but he felt tired: very tired. He had drunk wine all afternoon with Eva and at one point he had wanted to make love to her very badly, but he didn't know how to suggest it, and she had not encouraged him. Perhaps her body was only for old men. Perhaps young men frightened her. And then he was too drunk to make love, and the moment had passed, and he had staggered to his old room and the China Doll had been there with yet another client in wild coital convulsion.

Paul had stared, aghast as her black silk clad legs waved at him over the solid carved bedstead, and her spider's eyes had flashed dark fire. Then he had remembered that he had been relegated long ago to the box room, and that he was lucky to get that – officially, he had been declared dead.

That was the trouble! Officially, he was dead. It was on all the records and his mother had a certificate to prove it. He wasn't a real person at all. Since the explosion he had not existed – and neither had Captain Kraft. Everything the Captain did, therefore, was fantasy: his army, his men, his plans – even his cell in the U Bhan. It was all a fantastic game.

And he, Paul? He was dead too: but the only game he played was to attempt to believe that anything mattered ... and to continue to look for something real.

At school he had sung Schubert's music and the words ran through his head ... "*As by a crystal brooklet ... I wandered on my way ... and there among the ripples, I spied a trout at play ... as here and there he darted as lively as could be ...*" Then the fish was leaping in confusion about the kitchen floor, while China Doll was riding it, and she was in her black silk stockings and high heeled boots with spurs, and she wore a black and scarlet corset, fastened very tightly, so that her breasts jutted. Her face was masked, and she had a spider, a huge, hairy spider, sitting on one shoulder. She carried a whip, a thin stock that was made from the dried penis of a Spanish bull as was the custom, and she was whipping the dogfish and it was screaming, its eyes goggling, and its mouth wide and gaping – coming at him.

"And there upon the rivage, with rod and line prepared . . . a skilful, crafty angler . . . into the brook he stared . . ."

He had been walking for days, or it could have been for weeks, through ruined fields: through fields where the skeletons of horses lay exposed to the rain, and through fields where the trenches still stank of the putrifaction of the flesh of Europe's young men. All that was youth and beauty and brains had lived and died in the rat-run mud, and all that was left at home to continue were the mad, the lame and the decadent. Some of the young and beautiful had returned . . . but they had returned with hollow heads and hearts.

Before him was a field of turnips. He pulled some out by their tops, and with his blackened nails he scraped off the dirt – the dirt that must have contained the blood of soldiers – and he gnawed the raw roots until the emptiness in his stomach was satisfied. Then he had walked on. A cow to milk, tethered by the side of the road would help, but for two days he had seen no cow. The milk was good and nourishing, and would give him the strength to continue. He wished he knew where he was going.

Then there was a beech wood, and he walked through it, scuffing the loam. It was too early for spring, and too late for the dead leaves of Autumn. He didn't know what month it was. He walked on, and suddenly he was up to his knees in water.

He stopped and raised his head. Before him stretched a vast expanse of water: it was moving very swiftly in the centre, but eddying around him where he stood. He looked to the left, then to the right. It was a river – a wide, deep river. He had walked into it without looking. A little way down stream was a fisherman peering intently into the water, his line at the correct angle, and his body very still.

"Oye!" shouted Paul.

There was no answer. Paul shouted again. "What is this river?" No reply. The rod suddenly flickered into life and the fisherman began to play the reel.

"*. . . Said I, 'tis vain your trying your art in waters clear, the fish your form espying will hide away in fear . . .*" The line bent, and the fisherman reeled furiously.

"I say," shouted Paul . . . "Where am I?"

No reply. "*. . . But skilful was the angler . . . with cruel delight, he stirred up all those crystal waters . . . and hid the fish from sight . . .*"

"Where is Germany?" Can you tell me where Germany is?" Paul shouted. He was still up to his knees in the river. His feet were numb, and the cold was creeping up to his thighs, but he scarcely noticed. After so many days or weeks endlessly walking, his feet burned and ached.

No reply. "*. . . The fish, by this deception, the enticing bait sought out . . . and I was left lamenting the fate of that poor trout . . .*"

The rod flicked up and dangling, was a large fish. It jumped furiously, then the rod was dropped back into the water as the fisherman prepared to play it into a net. It was too heavy for the rod alone.

"Please . . . will you tell me . . . WHERE AM I?" Paul screamed.

The fisherman turned round wearily. "The Rhine . . ." he said. He pointed . . . "And that is the way to Germany . . ."

"I thought this was Germany?" Paul shouted.

"No. This is my property. A lot of things used to be Germany. But this is mine I am French – Salut!" And he turned away.

The dream left Paul wide awake and exhausted. It was the first time before dawn that he had a crashing hangover. Tomorrow, he would look for Cilly. He suddenly decided that he loved her. He wasn't sure at what particular moment he had decided that. Perhaps it was when he had returned to the box room and looked out and seen the window of Cilly's room, and realised that he had loved her all the time.

With Cilly by his side, things would be different. He would get a job   a real job   one that he would be proud of, and then he would start to put his mind back together again. Germany needed whole young men, not misfits. Things would never be the same   but perhaps, in time, they would be better.

* * * * *

THIRTEEN

For the third night in a row Paul was sitting in the club. He sat from early evening through till the last note had been played, the last drink drunk, the last customer, but himself, shovelled out on to the sidewalk. He watched the evening ebb and flow. He saw the early-comers followed by the more and more sophisticated. The most sophisticated were those who could judge their entry to the very second. The second at which the inner golden glow of the club exploded into a positive shining aura.

They came in on the highest of high tides and left when the tide was turning. The 'life' was really a being in its own right. It fed on the early arrivals, nourished the very chic, and slumped into near collapse like diseased lungs when the night was over.

Outside the club, the hoardings telling prospective clients that 'Iya Taboo' was singing inside were still up. This meant that for the three nights that he had been there, Paul had listened to the frequent apologies from the MC who regretted that their songbird of wickedness was no longer with them but that . . .

"She had gone to HOLLYWOOD!"

Then would come the last bitter dregs of the night when the transvestite owner of the gold mine would sing Brahms Lullaby to the few remaining drunks. The song always provoked tears though Paul could not be sure they were not tears of laughter for Viola was not a pretty sight and certainly not like anybody's mother. The cheaply powdered face, already looking like a detailed map of a mountain range when the club opened, took on a grotesque life of its own by three in the morning. The black beard showing through the dead white French chalk, the lip rouge smeared around the rims of a hundred glasses, the mascara like two shiners, and the whole thing topped by a cheap, ragged blonde wig. Not a pretty sight, at all.

'So good night boys and girls, good night," Viola husked when the lullaby had croaked to an end. "Thank you for coming. See you all again very soon."

He looked over to where Paul was sitting and smiled forlornly, then came across: "My, you are the persistent one, aren't you?" Paul looked up at him. "I keep telling you and everybody else that the little lady has vanished to America. Hasn't it sunk in, yet?"

"But why would she go without even saying goodbye?" Paul asked fretfully.

"It's women, my dear . . ." said Viola, getting confessional and cosy. "It's women . . . You shouldn't trust them . . . Find yourself a nice boy – you know what I mean?"

Paul did indeed know what was meant – he cast his mind back to Herman and his military amour: "She was different," he said, defensively.

"Different my ass!" Viola said. "They're all alike – what about that Prince, eh?"

"He came with the house."

"Balls! The house came with him, you mean. Listen Paul, she didn't give a shit about you and the sooner you get that through your preetty leetle head, the better. Well," he said, standing up, "this won't get any beds made or pisspots emptied. Goodnight, angel."

"Goodnight," said Paul as Viola moved away.

Viola's place at the table was taken by the handsome, well dressed man from three nights before – the one who had eyed Paul with such interest.

"Maybe," thought Paul, "this is the boyfriend Viola thinks I ought to have."

The first words, however, altered Paul's opinion. The young man's speech was as elegant as his clothes and his mode of address was civility itself: "Good evening. I have the impression that we have perhaps met before?"

Paul frowned – half to refute the suggestion, half in pretence that he was thinking about the possibility.

"Lieutenant von Lipzig. The Academy . . . Class of 1917 . . ."

Paul really couldn't remember; though that was his class: "Von Lipzig . . . ?"

"Yes, now I'm stationed at the Eden Bar . . . Baroness von Semering's regiment, you know?"

Paul did not know and could not for the moment think

that such a regiment existed: "Which regiment?" he asked.

The question produced polite laughter in his new-found classmate: "The Baroness von Semering's band of willing volunteers. It's a really very pleasant selection of men. The pay is very good and the uniform is more than stylish. Are you free now? You look free."

Paul gazed around the empty club and stared at his single glass: "How very observant of you," he said.

"Well, then, I wonder if you would be so kind as to give an ex-alumni a helping hand. You see, I seem to have this slight problem . . ." he nodded towards a darkened alcove where Paul could now make out the shape of two women. ". . . my slight problem is that my lady companion has, without prior warning, brought along a friend. Well, normally, you understand, it would be of little difference to me but this evening I am feeling just a little . . . how shall I put it? . . . anaemic. Yes, that's the very word. Anaemic   not enough blood for the both of them so if you would do me the great service of joining us at the Eden . . ."

Paul glanced again at the two women and then hauled himself to his feet:

"Why not?" he said. "Why ever not?"

"Capital," cried von Lipzig. "Splendid fellow!" He brushed his already immaculate jacket as the two women rose and came towards Paul's table. Paul could see that they had money. They were dressed fashionably, though overly so, so that they could not be described as chic. They were also running a little to fat though there were the remains of a certain flashy style of beauty. They were more than mature but at the moment acting in a somewhat girlish manner which could only be described as macabre.

Von Lipzig introduced Paul to them: "Frau Aekerle and Frau Smidt, may I introduce an old friend of mine, Paul von Przygodski."

The introduction was followed by much smiling and a little coy giggling and Paul found that he did not mind. Did not mind that they were slightly common and rather physical. He did not mind that he was marked as an ancillary to their night's fun and laughter. He did not mind, because he did not care.

"The Eden, God bless it," said von Lipzig.

"The Eden!" the women echoed and managed to add overtones of delicious vice and voluptuous goings on.

"The Eden," said Paul, and felt like a stick in a flooding river, carried along but not minding, and not in the least interested, as to where he would fetch up.

The Hotel Eden was everything that the Lützower was not. Its private club was dark and romantic where necessary but Paul could guess that, exposed to a bright light, it would still be clean.

There was a bar across from the dance floor and it was on to the dance floor that Frau Aekerle quickly manoeuvred him. She clung to him as he moved in rhythm to the music. The Prussian stiffness left him and he felt a fluidity which was alien to everything he could remember but the sensation pleased him. It was also very obviously pleasing his dancing partner who had put her head on his shoulder in the most intimate way and was now brushing her lips against his neck. It did nothing for him but neither did it offend.

They danced on, he fluid and mechanical, she imagining the movements of his lithe body were in direct response to her physical charms. Paul glanced down at her and she caught the look and smiled like a sexual conspirator but he was a million miles away and could not even have found himself.

They clung together as they lazily circled the floor. To the onlooker, despite the glaring difference in age, they made an interesting couple.

To the Baroness von Senering, it was only Paul who held any interest.

The Baroness' table cast its own glow over the proceedings. It was a little kingdom in its own right and the Baroness, on her tiny Gothic throne, was the kingdom's ruler.

She was a woman of uncertain age and immaculate appearance, a flawless almost pure look about here, and eyes that could pierce the gloom of the most difficult soul. A woman who long ago had come to terms with the world and who now knew the cost and worth of every living thing and of quite a few inanimate items as well. A woman who could turn the world's cynicism against itself, who constantly bid her hand to its exact value and for whom her ace was always trumps.

The bodyguard to her small but tentacled kingdom was a bevy of masculine beauty and sex appeal. Dressed by Kautz and with the morals of well groomed alley cats. It was their pleasure to wait on the Baroness and see that her every mood was catered for and her every whim was satisfied. She sat, flanked by this galaxy of bedroom stars, sipping champagne from a goblet made for an 18th century Doge, and watched Paul dance with the hawk-like interest of a Master from the Bolshoi.

She had seen him enter the Eden with Von Lipzig, who was a particular favourite of hers. Now she made a slight movement in his direction and the young nobleman immediately answered her call. He bowed: "Baroness?" he said.

"Your friend – I should like you to present him to me," it was an order given in the firmest and most attractive voice.

"Certainly, Baroness," he answered, and turned back across the room on his errand.

Paul was still a million miles away when he felt the tap on his shoulder. He stopped the dance in full flight and turned his head.

"Excuse me, Frau Aekerle," von Lipzig said. "Paul, the Baroness would like to see you for a moment."

"Me?" asked Paul, but followed his new-found friend anyway. He followed him across the ballroom and into the bar, through a crowd of smooth young men in formal evening clothes who eyed him with a mixture of envy and amusement. Followed him until he found himself being introduced to a woman with magnetic blue eyes.

"Baroness von Semering, this is Paul von Przygodski."

The Baroness raised her velvet-gloved hand and Paul bowed low over it:

"Come into my circle," she said. Paul did not answer.

"Champagne?" she asked, and waved a hand. Von Lipzig supplied Paul with a goblet of sparkling wine.

"It's Dom Perignon," she said. "My favourite." Still Paul

could think of nothing to say.

"Dancing, music, and champagne. That's the best way to forget everything. Forget until there is something worth remembering, don't you agree?" Her eyes were on him, studying him, waiting for his response, but none came. She wore a veil; her hair was blonde and smooth. She looked boyish but not masculine. As they faced each other, the onlookers were struck by their remarkable similarity – he was a strange reflection of her, and she of him. Like angels, they had a look of untouched purity.

"You dance well, you know, but I should say you have a military education. Am I right?"

At last Paul found his tongue: "Yes," he said. "Yes, that's right." And then, for no very good reason, he added: "My father is Colonel Przygodski."

"And languages?" she asked. "Do you speak French?"

"Somewhat, Baroness. I seem to have spent a great deal of time in France in one of their hospitals and . . ." he stopped, realising that this woman was interrogating him.

The Baroness sensed his uneasiness and smiled: "Why, you are wondering, am I asking all these questions? Let us call it an interview." She was smiling to herself: "Yes, an interview prior to a recruitment in a very dashing regiment of the line. *Recruitment* . . . that is the word, isn't it?"

"Yes," said Paul. "Yes, I suppose it is the word."

"And tell me, what is your rank?"

"Lieutenant."

"Well, Lieutenant," she said, very softly and almost kindly, "I am the sort of Commander-in-Chief of a regiment – a regiment of gigolos."

Paul was conscious of the words and conscious that the music out somewhere behind him was rising in a soft crescendo like the music for a dramatic operatic scene.

"Does that shock you?" she asked and he shook his head. Nothing really shocked him anymore. "It is a fine profession for the man with fantasy and fantasy of expression. Oh, I cannot abide a man who has no fantasy in his speech. It lacks charm. You have charm, haven't you? Yes, I can see you have."

"Charm and fantasy and good looks. That is what a

woman wants. Why, every woman knows that men can be strong and blunt and brutal. It is natural for every woman to know for nearly every woman has to suffer it. But when a woman is allowed her very own choice of a companion, why should she choose the same, dull thing? "You do not answer. That is because I know you could never be dull."

Paul was flattered though he wasn't sure if it was the sort of thing he should be flattered by. "I do not," she continued, "I do not say that at times even the dream prince should not be just a little forceful, a little demanding but only when the force and the demands are from the fantasy as well. You understand? I'm sure you do.

"Now I see you and I enlist you. You will be very comfortable among us. The tasks must be performed with an eye to detail and with dedication ... but isn't the task of making a woman happy for a few hours worth a little dedication?"

Paul nodded. He would agree with anything she said. The voice, as well as the blue eyes, were magnetic – hypnotic.

"And the rewards," she said, waving a hand to von Lipzig again, "the rewards, dear Lieutenant!"

From the small table next to the Baroness's throne, von Lipzig produced a silver casket and handed it to Paul: "Oopen it," commanded the Baroness. "Open it and take what is inside."

Paul lifted the lid and saw a bundle of clean currency. More money than he had seen in a very long time.

"It's yours," she said, "and tonight your fantasy and your charm and your dedication are for Frau Aekerle. She will be very happy, I am sure. Go now, Lieutenant. Do your duty!"

Paul looked at her for a moment, then he took the money and bowed. As he turned to leave, the phalanx of gigolos around Baroness von Semering, broke up and drifted away in little groups or singly. Paul looked back over his shoulder to see that the Baroness, sitting alone now, still had her blue eyes fixed on him. He straightened his shoulders, though in not too Prussian a way, and walked towards Frau Aekerle.

"You're all mine tonight," she giggled.

He hesitated for a moment. From all around he could sense that the other gigolos, von Lipzig, and, most of all, the blue-eyed Baroness were watching him with interest. He relaxed again and gave the lady his warmest smile.

"Yes," he said. "What a pleasant evening it has been and what a pleasant time we have ahead of us. Shall we dance? I love to dance with you."

Outside the Hotel Eden in the wide Platz there is a monumental column dedicated to some semi, and long-forgotten, hero. It is hollow and its stem has been drilled to make spy holes through which Herman and his men are able to follow the frantic comings and going of the Eden's clientele. Given more imagination on the part of his underlings, Herman could have known of all the professional couplings which were taking place in the city since the Eden was the brightest spot in the darkest day for many a rich widow and many a bored wife.

This set of spy holes was one of a series all over the town which Herman used to collect information on what he called the *'degeneration of the people'* and sometimes, even, the *'de-Germanification of the German people'*.

The communist cells were watched, and the *maisons* were watched, and the unions were watched, and the gigolos were watched. In that the gigolos believed in sharing the wealth of others, and in that they formed a brotherhood and in that they believed in fighting for basic rates for the job, they were like the other three rolled into one.

That thought was a little too deep (as were most thoughts), for Herman and he, despite the veneer of hardness, had a touching innocence, not to say stupidity, about him. All of which led to a great sense of shock and shame when, from his hidey-hole, he saw that one of the degenerates leaving the Eden as dawn was breaking was his old comrade-in-arms, Paul von Przygodski.

Frau Aekerle's apartment was rather like herself – slightly overblown and somewhat overfurnished. The moment they were inside the door, she made a lunge for Paul which, while not entirely unexpected, was a long way from the gliding, giggling part she had acted out in public. If he were to avoid probable bruises and possible concussion from her wild thrashing, Paul knew he would have to take the situation firmly in hand.

"Frau Aekerle," he said, firmly.

"Brunhilde," she said.

"Brunhilde . . . let me take it all in. You . . . in this perfect setting. The real you. Calm . . ." he dodged a body lock, ". . . tender . . . romantic."

It was no good. He was backing across the room and would soon be trapped in an alcove. The Baroness' words about sweet, fantasised love went out the window. With no thought to anything other than self-preservation, he reversed the roles and counter-attacked.

"Hilde! Hilde!" he shouted. "Give me your all. Give me every part of yourself! Now! Here!"

Frau Aekerle, though her head was lost in the raging battle, quickly saw that here was no place to undo her stays: "Paul, Paul!" she gasped. "The bedroom! My bedroom!"

Keeping up his whooping noises of flashing passion, he followed the routed enemy into a gilded room and on to a high, overstuffed bed. The nervous client lowered the lights and started to undress. Paul gave her a moment and then drew her onto the bed. It made him seem eager which more than satisfied the lady. "I can be rough with fantasy, too," he thought.

When she was finally naked and lying on the bed, he took his own clothes off like a professional lover and slid onto the bed. She was not unpleasant to the touch, and for all her years' advantage over Paul, she knew nothing. It was easy for him, with a natural ardour of physical response and the knowledge that the silver casket could keep him from having to ponder his aimless existence, to plunge into his task – which was Frau Aekerle – and dedicate his bodily movements to her satisfaction and his own, while allowing his mind to gallop off on all manner of wild goose chases.

Frau Aekerle, unlike the other two women in his life, expected nothing from this physical encounter since that was the sum total she had ever had from her previous physical encountered with the late Herr Aekerle.

Imagine, then, her surprise when, apart from the usual pleasant, warm sensation which she took to be the sole result of coupling, the lady had a reaction of volcanoc proportions which left her gasping and floundering on top of the bed long after Paul had slid between the sheets and dropped off to sleep.

Paul was still half asleep when he next found himself attached again to the ubiquitous Frau Aekerle. His semi-conscious state made it easy for him to perform and even if it was in a perfunctory manner, she seemed satisfied. Paul wondered whether his fee did in fact allow her two bites at the same cherry. He must check on that.

She smothered him with wet kisses, as, finally, he dressed, along with a series of coy smiles, some frightening sexual innuendoes and the promise of a present that would always remind him of her. He assured her, as he left at dawn, that he would never, ever forget that night.

A lot of his fee went on clothes at Kautz, as instructed by the Baroness. He was amazed how quickly his eye could choose the styles and colours which would make him most attractive to his potential clientele. He was impressed, too, by the speed at which the pretty and preciously over-scented assistant to the great master of Berlin, Paris, London, realised exactly what this young man's profession was.

Dressed in new togs and coiffed, polished and buffed, Paul sauntered along the main thoroughfares. His elegant progress did not go unremarked and, to his amazement, it seemed that many of his future possibles already knew of his alliance with the von Semering clan. "Berlin, the great capital . . ." he thought, "and Berlin . . . the tiny village."

Outside one elegant cafe sat two women who had seen him with Helga and wanted him then. Now they still wanted him but with his elevation into the official and expensive circle, were no longer sure they could stand the pace. As in all situations, they bit the hand that had not, as yet, caressed them.

"He's a gigolo," said Frau von Putzdorf. "Do you hear? A gigolo – while his poor mother still works in a turkish bath to make ends meet."

"They have no consideration for their elders, these young

people," said Frau von Uexkull.

"How true. Standards are deteriorating. Oh, where is the Kaiser?"

"Unlikely to return, dear," Frau von Uexkull said, and silently thanked God and the Allies. "Alas! All the young men. What are we coming to?"

"Shall we make a stand?" asked Frau von Putzdorf, and had visions of attacking all the eligible young men around and dragging them into dark, secret places equipped with manacles and large beds.

"A stand? In public? I hardly think so, dear!"

The Eden had an electric atmosphere that night. It was bright and gay and all the body of pleasing young men were happy. They were dancing, some with each other, and drinking magnums of champagne. They were clapping their hands like flamenco dancers and throwing the yellow dahlias from the vases on the tables.

It seemed to Paul that the place was *en fete* and that it had something to do with him joining the fold and proving to be a successful member of the clan. He drank glass after glass of wine and let himself be carried along in the wild, exciting mood which had enveloped the place. He had not felt so gay and irrepressively happy for as long as he could remember.

At the very moment when he felt that nothing could pop his balloon or prick his bubble, he looked up across the room to see that sitting at a table, and making signs that he should join him, was Lothar, one of Herman's helpmates. They made signals to each other and at last Paul made it clear that he would join him out in the loo. When he joined him there, he had another boring surprise – standing at the urinal and trying to look as if he were emptying his bladder, stood Herman in his brown leather coat.

"Herman!" said Lothar.

Herman turned his head away from the porcelain while carrying on the charade of micturation.

"Hello, Paul," he said. "We've been watching you."

"Really?"

"Yes," answered Lothar, "and we're a little disappointed. We had high hopes of you, Paul."

"Really?"

"Yes," said Herman, "we're a little disappointed. We held out great hopes for you. We thought you cared for the Fatherland but it seems you prefer escorting elderly ladies around luxurious places."

"I see your choice of venue hasn't changed much," Paul answered.

"We shall get you in the end! I shall get you in the end, Paul," said Herman menacingly — but it is difficult to be taken seriously when your dick is hanging out and you are fumbling to get it back in and buttoned up. Herman fumbled a little more and got the member out of sight.

"Mark my words . . ." he said, and left the loo just before Paul got a fit of the giggles.

The days that followed were almost indistinguishable, one from another. They all mainly began around a late lunchtime followed by a little expensive shopping and tea in the latest 'in' tea shop. After an interlude of Darjeeling and gossip, scandal and daydreams, it was home for a rest, a hot bath, a starched, snowy shirt and a precisely tied bow tie. The hair brushed till it gleamed, a squirt of Imperial cologne, a handkerchief flicked into place, a gardenia chosen for the buttonhole, the putting on of accoutrement which came from the memory of nights of love — cufflinks, gold watches, dress studs, chains, alligator billfolds, signet rings.

The days were all much of a muchness, the only difference was that with the changing of the seasons, an overcoat might or might not be worn, umbrellas might or might not be opened against the rain. Taxis were always taken.

All over Berlin, as in Paul's apartment, the evening ritual took place as Baroness von Semering's young and able bodied men made ready for the night. In the apartments of the aggressively masculine, the car keys of a smart, imported Bugatti or Dusenberg might be part of the clinking rewards put into lovingly cut barathea trousers; in others, the most treasured love tokens could be a piece of Tiffany glass or a Picasso painting.

Many of Paul's love tokens were still in their original jeweller's cases in his handkerchief drawer. A lucky burglar would have a field day if he opened it.

The Baroness's clients made few, if any, demands on their hired lovers' intellects. They did not go to the opera or the play, they did not go to concerts, they did not read the serious newspapers, they did not read the latest books. Their conversations did not demand thought or wit. Funny for the moment, blatant compliments, the discussion of the latest torrid love affair of this or that public person, laughter and, more often, giggling; dancing, groping and rubbing. The tango was their metre and champagne, the universal intravenous drip.

The Eden was the chosen stomping ground.

Before the Eden, there was often the private little cocktail party and the *diner intime*. These little extravagances on the part of former bed mates were feminine gestures, flutters at romance rather than a prior booking for the night to come. Every man was the favourite on the night.

The nights were often a haze for Paul. The music was internal, now, and the engine was lubricated with fine wine and fuelled by food which was *haute cuisine* by the grosser Bavarian standards.

From the first he felt that the money would be the passport back to the white clouds of non-thinking, no puzzlement, no thought for tomorrow and no recollection of yesterday.

And every move from waking in a strange bed or in his own if he was not chosen ... which was infrequently, was an onward move towards the Eden again. The scented battlefield where the weapons were words and slights, and the victories counted in wounded *amour propre*. Over it all, like a beautiful, unmoving and unmoved money spider ruled the blue-eyed Baroness. Her word was law. She was a divinity among the demi-gods of the Eden – the men who ruled the dance floor and the bedroom and who, by any standards would be lepers in other spheres if they cared to notice – took their orders from this unbending woman. They took their orders and their wages and loved every minute of it.

* * * * *

FOURTEEN

Paul had a call to tell him to be early that night at the Eden. It was the Baroness: "I have in mind to be a little more international," she said.

"When he got to the Eden, she had not arrived but there were three other of his colleagues at the bar. They, too, had received a telephone call along the same lines. They were excited.

"What do you think she intends?" one of them asked. He was very blond. Paul noticed that they were all very blond.

"Whatever it is, it will be exciting. How I adore the woman. What do you think, Paul?" he asked.

"I haven't an idea. Perhaps a network of Edens across Europe. London?"

"But who speaks English?"

"Who speaks French?"

It seemed that they all did, to a greater or lesser degree. It looked like France.

The Baroness arrived in a cloud of black velvet and a gust of Russian Leather by Chanel. Always a forceful person, even in repose, this evening she was particularly dynamic. She gave off sparks and the already excited young men buzzed with enthusiasm.

The Baroness took her seat in the alcove on the little Gothic chair and crossed one elegantly booted leg over the other. Klaus brought a huge ice bucket which was already prepared and glistening with condensation. In it, dark and beautiful was a magnum of Dom Perignon. She waved a hand at Paul and he lifted it gently from the bucket and wrapped a linen cloth around the neck.

A little working and the cork popped. Before the fine spume had chance to dissipate even a fraction of the pale golden liquid, he had deftly filled her goblet which another hand passed to her and had filled the other four glasses. The Baroness waited till each of her young men had their glass and then she raised her own: "Gentlemen," she said,

"Paris!"

Although they had all guessed that Paris was to be their

destination, the confirmation coming from her lips fired them anew. And, though they were too collected to show it, they were all, except Paul, very curious to know what she had in mind.

"It's a new world," she said. "Nothing which we once took for granted remains. Kings are in exile, old orders pass away, empires die and the barbarians at the gates take on the form of money changers.

"Well, everything changes but this is all taking place so quickly that we must be careful not to be left behind. We cannot afford to be parochial, can we?"

She offered up a glass for a recharge while they stood about her, and agreed that they could not indeed afford to think small.

"And so we must spread our wings and look for pastures new." She was smiling, making fun of her own words. "You see, darlings, when all the world has become one vulgar market place, and money is the only qualification for *entrée* into even the most exclusive circles, and when sex is no longer a private thing, then we are the last people in the world who can afford to be stuffy.

"And so we are going to Paris. We will show the ladies there that life is not one series of brutal apache dancers or lines of languid young men unable to fulfil their real role in life and love. We will show them that elegance and romance can go hand in hand with masculine strength, and that masculine strength doesn't mean being dragged all over a dance floor."

The Baroness's face was aglow with fervour. Her eyes seemed already to be watching rich, lonely ladies taking tea at the Ritz in the Place Vendôme and unhappy widows waiting forlornly for a half breed Algerian to come home to bed.

"I am making all the arrangements," she said. "Each of you will need new luggage and clothes. You buy what is required and have the bills sent to me."

"When do you expect to leave for Paris, Baroness?" asked Paul.

"We leave in a week's time," she said. "The Berlin–Paris express. It is all arranged."

Paul packed his new clothes into his new suitcases with some care. His wardrobes now were fuller than ever – different suits for different occasions but all of them a part of his uniform, though. His war now was one of survival and not of honour.

He dressed himself in a severe travelling suit and brushed his hair till it gleamed like a platinum helmet. He gave another pull to his tie and looked in the mirror. The blond Prussian about to take Paris by storm . . . just as they had done in the last century and singularly failed to do in this.

The station was alive with people, not all of whom were travelling. There were an extraordinary number of Brownshirts around. It looked like a rehearsal for a military coup. They stood in their groups and the city police and the railway police stood in theirs not enemies but very uneasy allies. The Paris express was standing at the station. Paul walked down the platform past the great steel and iron engine. Its fires had already built up the head of steam necessary to launch the luxury train on its way and the excess steam was kept in check by safety valves which kept sending white clouds across the platform. Paul walked through one without noticing. White clouds were second nature to him.

The porter found the car they would be travelling in and showed Paul to his seat and then brought the gleaming suitcases on board. He wished Paul a pleasant journey and Paul gave him a very large tip. When the porter left, Paul got up and went back on to the platform to wait for the others.

He was early. Strange that he was either early or completely vanished.

All around him was the bustle which goes with international departures. Poor families struggling down the platform to the third class compartments, laden down with bundles and bulging suitcases held in place by pieces of string, trailed after by thin-faced children with running noses. First class passengers, like himself, with their maids and manservants. Stewards and cooks seeing the last of the provisions on board, loading up the galleys with meat and fruit and vegetables. The noise of trains pulling in and out, people and whistles and above it, and still some distance away, the sound of gunfire again. Up in the main part of the station concourse Paul watched the groups of Brownshirts begin to move towards one another. Herman was up to his tricks again.

The other men began to arrive and five minutes before the train was due to leave, they saw the Baroness sweeping down towards them. The black velvet dress looking like a riding habit, black leather boots and a black, veiled hat, all surmounted by a fantasy of a black Russian sable wrap. Behind her, struggling to keep up with her elegantly but dominantly forward stride, came two porters with a trolley piled high with trunks and cases. She stopped and watched them while they piled the larger items into the luggage van and pointed to the things she needed on the journey. Then the little band resumed its forward march until she came up to her young men: "Good morning, darlings," she said. "Paul, give them something."

Paul handed over another large tip and they turned to board the train. At that moment, people began to scatter and the sound of gunfire was suddenly ominously close. People who were already hurrying to catch the train now broke into frantic runs. The Baroness paused at the foot of the steps into the compartment. "Oh, those people," she said.

Down the platform, hurrying as fast as a tightly hobbled skirt would allow, came a woman whom Paul had noticed several times in the Eden but had never spoken to. When she saw the Baroness, she tried to regain her composure: "Good morning, Baroness," she said.

"Good morning Frau Heinkerman. Paris?"

"Yes, I . . ." another clatter of gunfire surrounded them, and Frau Heinkerman dived on to the train without another word.

The train pulled out from the station in a cloud of steam and a hail of bullets. As they settled themselves in, the liveried steward brought them champagne and glasses. The Baroness sent the glasses away and produced her own from a tooled-leather box. The glasses bore the Hapsburg crest, Paul noticed, but said nothing.

Underneath the elegant exterior of the party, there bubbled an excitement such as a group setting off on a safari might feel. It was an outing, an adventure which they could all enjoy safe in the knowledge that the Baroness would protect them from all harm.

As the train gathered speed, they settled down to contemplate the great possibilities ahead. "Do you know Paris well?" one of them asked the Baroness.

"My dear," she said, "I have known it all my life. You will find it a beautiful city. A city of pleasure."

Paul looked at his glass and wondered what sort of life the Baroness had led before the Eden. He conjectured that whatever life it was, it must certainly have been one in which she had always known what she was doing.

There was a knock on the door and Frau Heinkerman came in: "I am sorry about the rush at the station," she said.

"My dear Frau Heinkerman," the Baroness smiled, her young men all stood up. "These really are mad days. What can one do except ignore these fools?"

Frau Heinkerman, who was still flushed from her dash and vaguely stimulated by the danger she had lived through, smiled back in agreement. "So you are all off to Paris?" she asked.

"And you, too, it seems."

"A small matter. I haven't been there since..." she stopped, afraid to give her age away. "I wonder if it has changed much."

"I doubt it," answered the Baroness. "The French are always the same... it is the visitors who add the glamour and sparkle. I understand that the Russian Grand Dukes are all restaurateurs and their places have been taken by the American millionaires. I expect that will make some difference."

Frau Heinkerman asked the Baroness if she would be lunching and it was understood that she would like some company. "Not me, but perhaps Paul, you would lunch with the lady?"

Paul, who had been rather looking forward to a restful journey, agreed immediately. "It will be a pleasure, Frau Heinkerman," he said. She told him her carriage number and left.

They all sat down again. "Paul," said the Baroness. "If she wants anything other than lunch, leave the settlement to me." It was the policy never to sully the young gentlemen with the commercial aspects of the business.

The dining car was a glow of pink lights, even though the sun was shining outside. The car moved with the motion of the train but it was a solid, safe motion. He remembered the last train he had been on the goods train he had taken when he left France. Something else reminded him of that journey Frau Heinkerman's face. It was slightly porcine both in formation and in colouring. He had collected her a few minutes earlier and she had made a great fuss about lunch. She was so pleased he was joining her and he must have whatever his heart desired. And so it went on as she took her seat at the table, and threw her furs over the back of her chair, and looked up at him through half-closed lids.

From her behaviour towards him, Paul knew that everyone else in the car except the very innocent (who might think they were mother and son), saw that their relationship was based on something other than mutual admiration. The others in the band were trained not to notice these looks. Paul noticed but simply did not care.

"What will you eat?" she asked him.

Paul was in no mood to make decisions: "Is there a set luncheon?" he asked the hovering steward.

"Certainly, sir. Here's the card."

"It doesn't matter," said Paul. "Just bring me the first item of every course."

The meat was delicious. It was white and soft and was bathed in a rich juice. He remembered the taste but could not remember the name. He asked the steward: "Fillet of pork, sir," he said. A little pink pig and a pink piggy woman. It was fantasy, of course, but he had finally eaten his pig and now he was to make love to the sow.

They drank raspberry liqueur which was colourless but filled with the essence of the ripe summer fruit. The restaurant car was a buzz of contented conversation and rich with the aroma of brandy, liqueurs and Havana cigars.

Frau Heinkerman made a great fuss, too, over paying the bill. She was vulgar and Paul had intentions of making her squeal. They left the table and Paul escorted her back to her compartment. He opened the door for her and stood back, giving the impression that he would now return to the Baroness.

"Won't you come in?" she asked. "I have a little flask of eau de vie. A *digestive* I'm sure you'll enjoy."

Paul stepped into the compartment and felt the deep pile carpet under his feet. The lady was in front of him and before she could turn to face him, he had put his arms around her and pressed her to him. She simpered with pleasure.

"Frau Heinkerman," he breathed into her ear. "What is this thing you do to me? Why do you excite me so much?"

In answer to these questions, she wriggled her body against his. "It is madness. Madness! I find you so desirable. What am I doing?"

"Do it," she insisted. "I understand."

He tried to slowly force her forward to the floor but the hobble skirt made the movement impossible: "Wait a moment," she said, and he released her. She went into her tiny bathroom and while she was gone, he drew down the blind and undressed himself. The sun against the blind made it possible to see inside the compartment but there was no glare. He heard little grunts coming from the bathroom as, he imagined, Frau Heinkerman struggled furiously to get out of her clothes. Then he heard what sounded like a little whoop of joy and the door opened. She was even more like a sow now that the supporting undergarments had gone. Her breasts hung down heavily as if she had charge of nourishing a litter.

"Come to me, my little piglet," he said. She looked a little puzzled at the remark but came nevertheless.

They stood locked together in a tight embrace while Paul let his imagination run riot. Finally he turned her around and forced her slowly to the floor.

* * * * *

FIFTEEN

The moment Paul stepped onto the platform, all the memories of France came flooding back to him. It was the smell of gallic tobacco and open urinals.

There was a great deal of fuss about the luggage. The George Cinq had sent its luggage brake to meet them but capacious as it was, there was still a little difficulty getting all of it inside. The porters began to grumble *sotto voce* until the Baroness gave them a curt, cold harangue in their native tongue.

"Remember," she said, "you can always insult the French as long as the tip is absolutely correct. By the way, there is never any point in over-tipping a Frenchman, he will not be grateful and he will think you a fool. You might also adapt that idea to all your dealings with these people."

From the taxi window, Paul watched the city unfold. He thought the traffic a deal more dangerous than the Brownshirts but he supposed every city had its cross to bear.

The George Cinq was a hotel on the grand scale. The hall was bigger in area than the whole of the Eden and off that there were vast public rooms. The place had a style that public buildings in Berlin lacked, it also lacked the Berlin air of decadence.

The men had rooms to themselves and after they had unpacked and changed they joined the Baroness in her suite. It was huge and very comfortable. Already it was awash with baskets of exotic fruit and ablaze with flowers. Paul wondered how her admirers had known she was coming. As they sat around and sipped champagne, people came and went and the telephone rang and rang. Some of the callers were men but the majority were women of a certain age and a flawless elegance. As the sun went down over the city, and the lights were turned on in the suite, the lamps reflected on the polished blond hair of the four young men. Though at the moment, most of the talking was between Baroness von Semering and her visitors, Paul noticed that their eyes for the most part were drawn first to the heads and then to the feet. Perhaps they were looking to see if this latest Prussian invasion had come, like the last, in riding boots.

They ate dinner in the hotel and moved on to a very dark nightclub in the Rue de la Paix. The Baroness was given a corner table and quickly made that and the nearby tables her own territory.

"Remember," she said to them, "you are available but mainly you are samples of what our fair country has to offer the world."

In a very short time, two of the Baroness's samples had vanished to other tables. Paul spotted them from time to time on the dance floor. He noticed their darker, French rivals looking at them with a mixture of curiosity and intense hatred.

The Baroness took it all in her stride. She was, perhaps, a little more animated than when sitting in the Eden, but who would not feel that sensation when setting out to conquer a whole new empire?

In between talking to visitors to the table, she talked to Paul, but though she told him many things and though he felt very much as one with her, she revealed no personal secrets. There was a line drawn, a demarcation which he guessed she had decided on years ago and had held to rigidly ever since.

Towards dawn, when the club was beginning to empty, Paul noticed a party of three men and one woman come in. The men were French, the woman was a beautiful negress: "She's American," the Baroness said. "She is all the vogue here, on the stage and in cabaret."

Paul could not take his eyes off her. She was dressed in a white, glittering dress and around her shoulders was a cloud of white fox. Her throat, her wrists and her fingers sparkled with blue-white diamonds. "She looks very rich," he said.

"She makes a lot of money and has many admirers. I doubt if she is rich the way you think, though."

"Is there a difference?" he asked.

"Yes," she said, "the very rich are seldom generous of their own accord ... they have to be given instructions. People who make a lot of money very quickly are often generous to the point of bankruptcy."

"I want her," said Paul.

"It is possible," she answered, correctly interpreting a

glance from the singer's table, "that she wants you, too. But it will have to be on my terms," she added, firmly.

Paul was awakened towards midday by the telephone standing beside his bed. He took a little time to focus and he picked up the receiver without speaking. It was the Baroness. "I have had a call from the singer," she said. "She wonders if you could meet her for an early evening drink at the Deux Magots."

"What's that?" asked Paul.

"A cafe over on the left bank. You'll like it – it's fun."

"About what time?"

"Five, five-thirty. See how you feel, darling."

"I feel tired," he said.

"You mustn't exhaust yourself," she said, laughing. "Have an easy afternoon. Call and tell me what happens."

Tired though he was, and slightly hungover, he was now awake and outside the window. Paris was waiting for him. He rang the bell for room service and then started to run his bath. He ordered coffee and fresh fruit and by the time he had drunk a cup and eaten a peach, his bath was ready.

The hot bath and the verbena soap made him feel better. He shaved carefully and splashed his body with cologne. Some fell in a delicate spot and stung a great deal. He rather enjoyed it.

He chose a dark blue suit and a pale satin cravat which was the identical shade to his eyes. His hair looked blonder than ever and when he checked his appearance in the mirror, he saw that the night's late hour had left no blemish.

He wanted to be beautiful for the beautiful negress. He wanted to give a lot of pleasure and get a lot of pleasure. He also assumed that he would get a lot of French francs as well.

He lunched lightly on fish and white wine and ate a sweet little apple tart. It was a world removed from strudel.

He walked along the Champs Élysées and looked back towards Napoleon's flamboyant victory arch. He was conscious of many admiring glances and not a few of dislike. Since the French had won the war, he couldn't understand what was bothering them. He noticed, too, that when he had a question to ask, the answers were curt and the defects in his pronunciation were pointed up quite rudely. He decided something which almost every other visitor to the city decides – he loved Paris but did not like its inhabitants. By quarter to five he had walked a long way and did not know where he was. He hailed a taxi and asked to be taken to the Deux Magots. As it happened, it was only a short ride and he was there just before five.

She was already waiting.

She sat alone at a table but every table around her was taken by men who were devouring her whole. There was no trace of wear or of fatigue from the late nights and the many drinks. She was, he judged, only a little older than himself.

"I'm sorry if I'm late," he said in French. "I didn't think you'd be here yet."

"It's all right to be here alone," she said. "Anyway, you're not late, I'm early."

"We both speak French with foreign accents," he said, and she laughed.

"Learned mine here at street level, what about you?"

"In a hospital."

They drank some anisette and talked and stared avidly at each other. All around them people stared at them and wished the German bastard was dead so that they could lay the beautiful nigger bitch. He read their thoughts: she knew them instinctively.

"I want you to come to the theatre tonight," she said. "Can you do that?"

"Of course. I'd love to."

"Great!" she said. "I've got to go back and rest now, I'll leave the ticket at the box office. You come backstage after the show."

Back at the George Cinq, he called the Baroness from the lobby. "Come up and tell me all about it," she said.

He went up and told her about his day and the arrangements for the evening. His colleagues were there, too, drinking cocktails and enthusing about the city and its prospects. He stayed a little while and then went to his room to change. He soaked in his bath and then put on a dinner jacket. He added a few touches of jewellery and went downstairs. He told the taxi driver to take him to the Odéon and relaxed in his seat.

The woman at the box office looked at him with interest when he asked for his ticket. She rang a bell and a Frenchman with a polished bald head came and showed him to a box which was almost on the stage. The theatre was crowded and soon after he had taken his place, the house lights went down and the curtains parted.

The first part of the evening were the warming up acts. Tumblers and trained dogs and French comedians who spoke too quickly and with too much slang for him to follow. He was not very amused.

In the interval the usher brought him a large glass of champagne and a note written in English which he could not understand. The writing was ill-formed and the paper a rather bright shade of mauve. The lights went down again and the curtains opened and there she was. Shimmering where she was clothed and glowing black where she was not, and surmounted over all with a great headpiece of ostrich feathers and rhinestones.

When she sang, he responded immediately. Her voice was thrillingly pure and her pronunciation was charming. She sang mainly in French but there were one or two songs in English. One which he could not follow was about a gigolo. He looked at her carefully while she was singing it but she made no gesture nor glanced his way and he guessed the song was not for his benefit. She finished her act with a song about Paris which the audience loved so much that she had to encore it. When she finished, the stage was deep in roses.

Backstage he was taken straight to her dressing room. The room and the narrow passage outside were thronged with people. When he finally got into the room, he sat down and waited until she had shooed the rest of them away.

"I won't be long, darling," she said. "I'll just change and then we'll go to dinner."

He hoped she would change in front of him so he could see all of her perfect body but with a modesty which baffled him, she went behind a screen.

They went to Maxime's where she seemed to know everybody. Their progress from the door to their table was slowed by a series of kisses and compliments. She seemed very used to the adulation.

She ordered dinner with enthusiasm but ate hardly anything at all. Silver dishes of tiny birds came and went away again, as did a truffled lobster and a fillet of beef in pastry. Paul ate enough to satisfy himself, though she would have had him eat more, and together they drank rather a lot of Bollinger.

She seemed to hold her liquor very well and, if anything, he was affected by the alcohol more than she was.

After dinner she produced a tiny gold box and took a pinch of white powder from it and sniffed it up her nose.

"What's that?"

"Coke, darling. Would you like to try some?"

"Please," he said, and took rather a large pinch.

She laughed: "That should set you up very nicely," she said.

Dinner was over and Paul was feeling fine. His singer was obviously having a lot of fun and her high spirits made her seem all the more desirable. He wanted to make love to her very soon and said so.

"Have to do my cabaret first, honey," she said. "Then I'm all yours."

He hid his disappointment and hoped that the cabaret act wasn't a long one.

She signed the bill and they left followed by the knowing glances of an older generation. The taxi ride was very short and took them to the back of a building which did not look at all attractive: "Don't let the look of the place fool you," she said. "This is the most expensive club in Paris."

Her dressing room was almost impossible to believe. It was a profusion of colour from the scarlet silk wall hangings to the massed bunches of flowers from a hundred admirers. The seats were all couches with Egyptian overtones, made for effect rather than for comfort. There were buckets of champagne on the dressing table as well as a pile of letters and telegrams. And the room was very, very hot.

Paul was already feeling a little dizzy from the drink at dinner and there was another sensation which he did not recognise at all. He was elated far and above any reason he could think of.

"How d'you feel now, darling?" she asked.

"Fine! Wonderful! Even better if I kiss you."

She came over to him and he measured her whole breadth and length against his own. He saw the contours of her body, more pronounced than was fashionable and more erotic than anything he had ever seen before.

She took him in her arms, looked at him for a second and then slowly put her open, wet mouth on to his. She stayed like that for a moment and then slid her mouth all around his while her tongue darted like a bird inside his mouth and licked around his nostrils. He felt sensations in parts of his body he had not till then knew existed.

He held her so tightly and so close that it felt as if they were already naked. There was no part of her body that he could not feel in detail. They clung together for several minutes while she went on and on with her kissing then she broke away.

"I've got to change and get out there but knowing you're waiting for me will give me every encouragement to make it the shortest act on record."

She took off her dress, this time in front of him, and put on the tightest, most brilliant dress he had ever seen. It was a mass of sequins and it clung to her body as if it were wet: "Can you just do up the last few hooks?" she asked. He stood there while she turned her back to him. It was a great temptation – he wanted to strip it right off her back. In time he remembered that in the final analysis, she was the boss.

She took another pinch of the white powder and an enormous gulp of champagne and went through the door. He followed her to the wings of the little stage and watched. Out beyond the curtains, people were eating and talking and making a lot of noise but as the curtains drew back without any introduction, the noise died right away to a breathless silence. Then the silence was broken by an approving roar of recognition and the wild clapping of hands. The white piano tinkled a few notes and silence returned. She opened her mouth and sang. Paul noticed that she sang leaning on a chair. It looked as if she was being sexy and slinky; he guessed it was to aid her balance after all the drink and drugs she had taken.

Song after song poured from her lips. She hardly waited for the applause for one to begin to die down before she had started another one. In spite of his urgent feelings, he was more than content to listen and look, safe in the knowledge that the lady was his for burning.

She finished, glided off the stage, almost ran back on, threw extravagant kisses and words to her fans and came off again, signalling to the stage hand to keep the curtain down. Then she had Paul's hand and was dragging him back to the lurid dressing room.

She was talking half in French and half in English: "Honey! Cheri!" and the lips were all over his face and the hands all over his body.

"Unfasten me," she said, and he tried to do it over her shoulders but it was impossible. Finally he had to be a little firm with her and make her turn around and stand still.

"That's right," she was saying. "You be masterful . . . You blond god . . . I'm your slave . . . You can do with me just about anything you want to . . ."

On top of the layer of passion which was engulfing him, Paul felt another wave of desire. He held her back for a moment then kissed her hard and bit her lips. She wriggled free.

"That's right, honey . . . You do that . . . I'm here just for your pleasure . . . What you want is fine by me . . ."

She was naked and he could look at her and feel her. The skin was like velvet and her breasts stood up and away from her body. He placed his hands over her breasts and spread his fingers to see the contrast of white against black. Her eyes were opening wider and wider. He marched her backwards towards one of the awkward couches and pushed her down on it.

"You're my slave?" She nodded. "I can do anything?" She nodded again. "And if you refused, I could rape you? And if I wanted to, I could tie you up and beat you?"

While he was talking and she was silently agreeing, he undressed himself.

He stopped in his labours for a moment to lean over her body and massage it firmly again. From every contact he got a shock which drove him nigh to distraction. The woman just lay and breathed deeply and stared with white, wide open eyes.

They met with precision and a force which made her gasp slightly. At the same time as he was covering her face with kisses, his hands were running over her body and he was moving with her in what already seemed a crescendo of passion which must explode at any moment.

His mind was a great, gaping void empty of everything except the sensation of her touch and the feel of her flesh on his own.

"You're my slave," he breathed.

"Yes!"

"Anything?"

"Yes!"

"Anything I want – anything at all!"

"Yes!"

Her voice rose to a scream and he heard his own breath coming in strangled gasps which threatened to engulf him. Then his body drained and drained and there were blinding flashes in front of his eyes and inside his head and it was all over bar the cheering.

He lay for a long time on her body, enjoying the feel of her and slowly recovering. She lightly touched him the way a mother lightly caresses her child's cold hands after a game in the snow. He could feel the present and taste the immediate past: she was at one with the world, the drugged fantasy over, the effect of the drug still strong.

When he got up, he turned immediately from her and when he looked back, he saw all the red satin flowing round her limbs. She looked like a black, bleeding corpse in a trench. Then he kissed her very gently and she smiled dreamily at him. "You were marvellous," he said.

"You were incredible," she answered.

She did not want him to take her home. She was floating on a high and he had not joined her. She was sensible enough to know that her languid, fulfilled state could be irritating to somebody who was not tuned in.

"I'll call you," she said.

"Please."

"I've made arrangements with the Baroness . . ."

He put his hand to her lips and then kissed her again: "But," she went on, "I want to give you a present and I haven't brought anything with me. Here," she said, "take this. Keep it as a souvenir or sell it and buy something wonderful. It came from a banking prince and it goes to a prince of fantasy."

It was a single strand bracelet made up of brilliant white, square-cut diamonds.

"Thank you," he said.

"No . . . Thank you!" she answered.

It seemed only seconds after he left her that desire swept over him again. He looked into his own mind very carefully and smiled with pleasure. To be outside of himself. It was a new dimension, but now, although he had an urgent physical desire, he had no fantasy, which was just as well, for it was late and the loucher ladies of the night had long since retired to bed.

He found a girl down by the river. She was a recent whore. Not well versed in her trade and with nowhere really to take her clients. She asked only a little money which he felt was caused by her nervousness. He wondered how to tell her that she was charging too little.

They went down the steps to the place where the fishermen sit and wait for their small catches and she lifted her dress.

She knew nothing and she was not, in herself, very exciting: but the mechanics of the encounter fascinated him and he had no difficulty in functioning.

She had tiny breasts, more like a boy. It seemed quite pure and natural.

When he had finished, he put his hand in his inside pocket and took out his wallet.

"You're not French, are you?" she asked: "Are you American?"

"Yes, I'm American," he said.

It was dark and he had trouble telling which notes were which. It didn't matter to him but he remembered the Baroness's strictures about over-tipping the French. At last he found the right amount and it seemed terribly mean.

"Here," he said, "here's the money . . . and take this." He

handed her the bracelet. "It's real and it's worth a lot of money. Sell it and go home. You can start your own little business."

She took it and stared at it and then at him. She looked curiously at the bracelet. She did not seem very impressed.

"Thank you," she said.

She gave another tug at her skirt to adjust it and ran off up the steps.

By the time he reached the George Cinq, he was eaten up with remorse. Gifts over and above payment were always the property of the lover but he should have been sensible. The gifts were insurance against the day when a face had been seen once too often.

He passed the door to the Baroness's suite. A light came from under it and he knocked gently. She came to the door, perfect to look at but slightly tight.

"Paul? How did it go?"

"It was great fun . . ." he said, ". . . but I've done a very stupid thing . . ." and he explained about the bracelet and the young tart: "I must be punished," he said.

She looked rather stern: "Frau Heinkerman mentioned something about that as well," she said. "What sort of punishment do you think you deserve?"

"I should be thrashed," he heard himself say from a distance. His stomach felt tight. Another part was saying: "Not me!"

"I'll tell you something, Paul," she said, and her voice was very cold so that it frightened him. "I am going to punish you but not because you gave a valuable bracelet to a girl, though, poor thing, she'll probably either give it away or be robbed by some cheap jeweller. No, I am going to punish you because you went off with a streetwalker and may have caught a disease.

"Can you imagine what would happen it you had, and you passed it on to one of our clients?"

He hadn't thought of it at all, but he nodded.

"Now go to bed. Tomorrow you go back to Berlin to see a doctor."

* * * * *

SIXTEEN

Sometimes, in the swansdown whirl of it all, Paul would remember things. A trusting little pig, or a moment before it all began when his father was as real as any Prussian soldier can be. There would be revealing flashes through the clouds when he would recall the time he could make a value judgement with the best of them. He suspected that there had been a time when he had pride as opposed to simply being proud. There was a suggestion that once he respected people and hoped they respected him. And occasionally (and often at the oddest times), he would remember Cilly.

But none of his memories marked him or gave his ego or his conscience a sciatic twinge.

The days and the nights passed in well heeled, glamorous confusion. Sex became mechanical the more thought he put into it. The more pleasure he gave, the less he took except in the pride of success. His dancing improved, his small talk was gauged to the meanest of dumb blonde intellects, his compliments were almost psychic in the ability he had to strike an unerringly right note.

His professionalism served all the more to cloak him from any winter thoughts but sometimes an icy shaft could break through. One broke through with the release of Cilly's first Hollywood film. Paul was not interested to see if she was a success in her newly chosen career, he was only interested to see if she was as he remembered her at that last moment, just before the lights went out.

She was the same, perhaps a little perter but that could be the part. He felt unmoved by her as she went through a series of song and dance routines high up on the flickering square screen. It was very one dimensional and he remembered the flesh. Her voice was higher pitched than in real life and thus slightly histrionic, which was not the way his inner ear had recorded her. And the clothes were garish without being fun . . . and Cilly had always been fun.

But the last production number broke through and the shaft was icy and cruel. It was unreal but none the less cutting for that. Cilly prancing down a column of gigolos deciding which one should favour her that night and singing some song in English which he did not follow but which sounded cynical. He wondered if she knew about him. If she cared to enquire of her Berlin friends, she would know. Was the scene of her own making?

He left the picture house before the final credits and stumbled into the foyer. There she was again on the placards, teasing and tantalising in scenes from the picture.

He was dazed. Outside the picture house he could hear menacing shouts and as he came to the door, Brownshirts, four abreast and arms linked together, marched up the pavement, forcing people into the road.

They were singing and shouting and beneath the swaggering bravado an observer saw there was threat and menace. Today vaudeville, tomorrow the world. They milled up the street with some passers-by objecting noisily and getting very short shrift for their pains, others, remembering students and cadets, and the playful camaraderie of the Prussian adventure, cheered them on.

Paul noticed them only because they were physically there, otherwise they did not penetrate other than as an irritant. He had his thoughts, sketchy though they were, in other realms. He was not proud of being a gigolo, yet neither did he mind. Gigolo or sewage worker . . . what was the difference? The sewage worker smelled bad, earned little and was even less sociably acceptable than he was, and yet somewhere he remembered that the labourer was worthy of his hire. Was he worthy of his hire?

The question nagged him all the way home and that was uncomfortable since the whole object was to feel nothing, care for nothing, despair for nothing – and most certainly not feel, care, or despair for himself! Philosophy was not Paul's strong point and no effort had been made to instil even the most rudimentary knowledge of the subject at the military academy – perhaps if there had been, the losing of the war might have been more acceptable: "Did we lose the war?" he wondered.

He pondered these things while he lay in the bath soaking. He had so lost the habit of thinking properly, or for the future – other than what he would eat or wear, that the pondering came and went in short, disjointed flashes.

While he was dressing in his penguin suit, he decided that his father would have the answer to all his half-formed questions. And if he did not have the answers because the questions were so vague or so unanswerable, then at least the Colonel would be able to approve his strategy for perfect survival in an imperfect world.

The Pension Przygodski was quiet for a change. The inhabitants were either preparing for the evening or already engaged in their business activities.

Paul found his father alone in the drawing room. He sat, as ever motionless and emotionless. He was a clock that had stopped in 1918.

"Good evening, father," Paul said. The Colonel remained the same; trapped in his immobile body. Paul looked at him very carefully, and slowly he felt that something had changed. The clock had chimed a silent quarter or something.

"What is it? Why are you looking at me like that?" he asked.

He knew the answer and he knew then that his father would not put his unformed questions into any sensible slot nor give him any reassuring answers. His father knew and, knowing, disapproved.

"Well that's just fine," said Paul.

"That's just fine and dandy, isn't it?"

His father sat like badly carved stone.

"Well, it's easy for you to talk, I suppose. Your lot had it right all along the line. You wanted war, famine and pestilence and you got war, famine and pestilence in quantities and quality beyond your wildest dreams.

"You didn't have to think. You just had to sit back in your chosen career and let it all wash over you. You became somebody. People cheered you on – they admired you, respected you and what for? All you did was take orders. It isn't as if you had to think for yourself or anything difficult like that!

"Huh! I thought strategy was something you learned to take in any and every eventuality. I should have known better when I first saw those stinking, mud and blood-filled trenches. It wasn't strategy, was it? It was a master plan that went wrong but which couldn't be abandoned because you had nothing to put in its place.

"Now look where people are who believed in that ... They're just as trapped as you are ... You don't approve but there's nothing you can do about it. And supposing you could? Supposing you weren't bound to that chair? Supposing you could stand up and tell them where they were going wrong? ... Do you really think you would? ... Or would you be like those bloody fools of Herman's, parading up and down the streets in daylight and hanging around lavatories and the like at night? ... Do you think you can change the world from a lavatory or by looking through spy holes or living in lice ridden, broken down railway carriages ...?

"Do you know what most people are doing these days? ... They're forgetting everything that ever happened. They're forgetting so hard that sometimes they wake up in the middle of the day and wonder what it is that they're making so much effort to forget! They've forgotten what it is they don't want to remember!"

Paul was so intent on driving home at the wreck of a man sitting in front of him that he did not realise that he was beginning to shout or that the door behind him had opened and Mutti had come in. She called him softly but he did not hear her.

"So I'm at the Eden," he said, fiercely. He waited lest there should be some reaction, some slight movement but there was none.

"Now I know what you'd say if you could *'It's not really the sort of life that you had foreseen for your son'* is that right? I mean is that it ...? Oh, I agree, it isn't really the sort of job that I'd like to walk down the street boasting about ... though many others would be glad and proud to be able to say it.

"But there it is, father. That's how it is.

"Your son is a gigolo and though he isn't proud of it, he doesn't very much care either. And do you know what ... not many of the people who you respected in the past care very much either.

"Gigolo or honest, starving patriot they just can't tell the difference and they don't care and, when they do care enough, they'll start another war . . . and this time I'll be right in the thick of it . . . I'll get my brains blown out and you'll be proud of me again.

"Don't worry, father, you'll be proud of me . . . just you see. The sins of the bedroom will be washed away in the blood of the next battlefield. You'll see."

The flood subsided. His father was the same and whether Paul's words had really reached him was of very little importance: in leaving Paul they had drained him in his tirade, he had taken away the last of his interest in the day to day living.

Paul turned to leave and saw Mutti standing by the door. He saw by her face that she had heard most of his speech. He saw by her face, too, that though she didn't understand the details, she understood the pain. The pain for which there was no known cure.

"Paul," she said, softly.

He stared at her and wondered if at any time, the love she had given him had been constructive: "Paul, you must get out of this country while there is still time," she said.

"I'm tired, mother. Talk to me another time. I'm tired and I think I'll go back to bed."

"Paul you must do something . . . anything to get out of here. If you haven't got enough money yet, save hard . . . don't spend it on silly things. Or marry a rich American it doesn't have to mean anything. Once you get over there, you can get divorced. Everybody does it!"

Even her considered ideas were outlandish and her seriousness funny.

"I'm tired, we'll talk about it another time," he said.

"You know Cilly's back?" she asked.

"Back in Berlin? Why?"

"She's come back to marry a prince," Mutti said, as if that explained everything.

"But I only saw her at the pictures this afternoon how can she be here?"

"She's here," said Mutti, "and she's come to get married."

"When?"

"Next Saturday – he's a prince, she tells me. Very rich and very handsome . . . just like a prince should be. She's a lucky girl, isn't she?"

Paul straightened up and smiled: "Yes, Mutti. She is just that and I think she always will be. But you'll see . . . I'll be lucky too and then you'll be proud of me . . . just as I was telling father." He kissed her and went out of the apartment.

She called after him down the stairs: "Good night Paul, and remember what I said – save your money or find a rich American. It doesn't matter how old she is as long as she's rich . . ."

Paul raised a hand in salute as he went down: "Good night, Mutti," he said.

"You can always get divorced," he heard her voice go on. "Nobody cares over there . . . Paul, I don't mind what you're doing . . . but this place is going to be dangerous. I've already lost your father and . . ." but he had reached the door and it closed over her words.

Paul walked slowly through the streets. He was not thinking of anything in particular or going anywhere in particular. The streets were a strange mixture of luxury and poverty. He looked as if he were on the side of luxury and he looked, in spite of the hall marks of his profession, like one of the rich. He looked through people the way the really rich can and he seemed such a long way above them that beggars did not bother to ask him for money.

* * * * *

SEVENTEEN

The front hall of the Eden was awash with luggage from Vuiton. Trunks and cases and little bags for this item on the journey and that item on arrival. A jewel case of ample proportions, hat boxes and wicker baskets, all with steamer tags on them, all with the first class markings from an expensive liner.

The pile grew as more luggage was brought in by the porters. The pile took on a personality of its own and told its own story. There were two people attached to it. A man with expensive, well worn luggage and a woman who had only recently pillaged the Paris store.

Along with the last pieces, Helga walked into the hall escorted by a very elderly, elegant man whose nose looked as if it had been broken in a boxing bout.

"Darling," she said. "This is the place."

"I usually stay at the Adler," he said. "Is this place up to it?"

"This place is up to anything," she laughed. She looked as stunning as ever. Her travelling clothes were pure Paris out of English tweeds and around her there was a waft of perfume which had commanded the skills of generations of perfumers.

The manager of the Eden stood waiting a little before approaching the expensive pair: "Senora, Senor," he said, "welcome, welcome to the Eden."

"Oh, Heini, Heini," Helga cried. "How good it is to be back."

"Lovely to see you again, Madam. May I say you haven't changed a teeny little bit."

"Flatterer, Heini! Heini, this is my husband, Senor de Ribatejo." She waved a hand at the old man.

"Delighted, sir, I am sure you will be very comfortable here. If there is anything you want," he snapped his fingers at the porters, "just ask." The porters began to collect up all the luggage and move it to the service lift.

"We have several things in mind, Heini, but I don't think they'll be too much of a test for you," said Helga. "The

Baroness will be here later?"

"Of course, Madam. As usual and as always. You have a special request for her?"

"It will keep," she said. "Now, let's have champagne up in our suite. Pink champagne, Heini. I feel like drinking pink champagne."

She flowed towards the passenger lift followed by her husband. The elegance of his movements and the beautiful cut of his clothes could not quite hide the fact that he was a very old man. Heini hoped that Helga's passionate nature would not prove too much for him. It was always unpleasant when guests died in an hotel. Hotels were for living and dancing and drinking pink champagne, not for death and widow's weeds.

But looking at the retreating figure of the lovely lady, he doubted that if death should come to pass, she would be wearing widow's weeds for very long.

The walk through the streets did not so much as clear Paul's mind as let him retreat trance-like back into his former state. Those things that had puzzled and hurt him only hours before sank under the ready-made blanket he had woven long ago and were held there, warm and comfortable but prisoners none the less.

Although earlier he felt tired, now he did not and as he came back to the present, he saw that his footsteps had taken him nearer and nearer the Eden. And duty called. The Baroness would be expecting him. He had a job to do.

"On parade," he thought, and turned his steps deliberately towards the door which led to his place of work.

He sat at the bar after saluting the Baroness from across the room. A slight wave of her hand told him things were well but it was not important to him to know with whom the evening would be spent. The other young men drifted in to take their places, some at the bar, some around Baroness von Semerling.

A few early arrivals had already claimed their escorts and some were dancing. The music, soft and easy, and the mood relaxed. No thoughts and no pressure, just an evening of pleasantries and pleasure, a little too much to drink, a little too much exuberance on the dance floor. It was very comforting and reassuring.

Paul sat and watched and waited. He watched the barman shake the cocktails and saw them spilled out into modern glasses. Violet cocktails and some rainbow-hued, others so pale they might be spring water and some chocolate brown with cream floating on top. The smell of turkish tobacco filled his nostrils and he knew that von Lipzig must be in the bar.

He heard snatches of conversation. The promise of a ring: "With my birth-stone!"

"Which is?"

"Sapphire . . ."

"Of course! Remember, the prettier the blue, the less they're worth. It's the almost black ones you want . . ."

Amazing the sort of information you could pick up here.

"I drew the line at riding with her. Three years in Vienna has ruined me for early morning hacking with that woman . . ."

Paul sipped his champagne and drifted off again. How could Cilly be in Berlin when he had seen her in the movie this afternoon? He wasn't making sense. The film must have been made weeks ago. Her part would have finished then and after that they would have to put it together. Maybe she came on the boat that brought the film.

"Another Alexander, Klaus."

"Yes, sir." Klaus said 'sir' as if he meant it. Perhaps he did.

"Do you really like that drink?"

"I don't like any drink."

Champagne made him feel just a little bit green inside some mornings. It wasn't supposed to give you a headache but it gave him one. Perhaps that was because of his war wound. What war wound? What war?

"She wants me to go for a whole month to the mountains what am I supposed to do there . . ."

"What do people do in the mountains . . .?"

"I seem to think they wear strange clothes made of that heavy green horse blanket material Bavarian peasants swirl around in . . . and they walk up the stupid silly things . . . and then they walk down again . . At least I can truthfully say I can't ski . . ."

"She'll be tired out by night, though . . ."

"Not her! And even if she is, she'll still expect it . . . After all, it's me who has to do the work . . ."

"God . . . sometimes it is work too, isn't it . . .?"

"No so bad as driving a tram, I suppose . . ."

It was not as bad as driving a tram. Driving a tram you had to think where you were going and be there on time and not kill people. You had to concentrate and concentration on one subject led to concentration on another.

Paul could dance and talk and make love and the only concentration he needed was so finely judged that his mind could be off elsewhere and that was mainly nowhere at all.

"You're lovely, Paul . . ." he would hear and he would hear his own voice answering just as if someone had put on the right gramophone record at exactly the right time: "So are you: Countess: Berthe: Marta: Frau Belinger:"

"I need you, Paul, . . ." a voice would say.

"I need you, too: Countess: Berthe: Marta: Frau Belinger:"

"The trouble with her is she dances so well she wants to keep on all night . . . I can't be doing with it . . ."

"Better than some of them – they want to talk all night . . . And they're so dull . . ."

"Dull or not, it beats sweeping the streets . . ."

But it wasn't dull. Things were always happening – little things, just big enough to add a dash of spice, not big enough to disrupt things. Like now, there was disruption if ever he saw one.

Helga and a very old man coming through the door. He did not stir too much for he knew it must be his imagination. Somebody who looked like Helga and who had come to the wrong place, else why bring a man – even an old one – with her?

She was stunning in a shiny frock that clung, a silver fox boa, and white feathers in her boyish hair.

He got up off his barstool and walked a little way towards the couple and then decided it could not be Helga and turned to walk back to his seat.

Helga saw him and turned to her husband: "There he is,

Tony. I'll be right back."

She called him: "Paul! Paul!"

He turned but did not go across to her and she was forced to come to him. He was surprised. His imagination had played him double false: "Helga! It is you!"

"Of course it's me. Darling, how good you look! Just the way I always wanted you to look."

"Did you?" he asked. "I knew there was something strange about you but I couldn't remember what it was."

"You vanished so completely."

"So I'm told, but I'm here now. Would you like to dance – I think you liked to dance, didn't you?"

She looked at him carefully to see if he was being bitter or making fun of her but there was no expression in his face and certainly no guile.

"You dance now, do you? I'd heard you were doing very well in your chosen profession and I wondered how you could be if you hadn't mastered the art."

"I dance," he said, and swept her onto the floor. He made no especial effort but he was good.

"You're good!" she said.

"You've improved a lot yourself. Who's the old man you came in with?"

"He's my husband."

"Any general we know?"

"He is not a general – he is not even German. If you really want to know he's Brazilian – Antonio Jose Felice de Ribatejo." She pronounced the names with a strong Spanish accent.

"Is he an ex-prize fighter? He looks like an ex-prize fighter. It must be that broken nose."

"He broke it playing polo a long, long time ago . . . If you are interested, he's a coffee grower . . . In fact he's got the largest plantations in the country . . . He is very, very rich."

"Interested? Why should I be interested?" he asked.

"Because it's his money which is paying your wage tonight . . . We're buying you all for ourselves," she said with a note of savage triumph in her voice.

"I'm afraid you can't buy me tonight. I'm already spoken for," he said.

"Yes, I know that. Suite 217. Our suite!"

"You make it sound as if you're buying a piece of meat in the market, Helga."

"Sweet meat, Paul. But don't be offended – after all, we have been very, very close friends in the past and I have seen to it that there is an extra thousand American dollars for you," Helga said. The savage triumph came again.

They danced on and Paul thought of Mutti and 'go to America'. A thousand American dollars. He wouldn't need a rich American. On the other hand, he didn't need America – any fears he had could not be got rid of by travelling.

"You mean to say that your husband is putting up the money so that you and I . . . ?"

She nodded: "That's right."

"Whatever for?"

"It's his own idea . . . almost. He desperately wants a son and heir . . . and he can't quite raise the prospect himself, you know?"

"All that polo?" he asked.

"Whatever . . . anyway, I persuaded him that the best thing he could go for would be pure Prussian blood."

"Thank you!"

"He wanted English, at first. But I persuaded him that I would be more at ease with a man I knew . . . and that Prussian was better. Well, only consider, Paul, it's not as if you and I were strangers. In fact, I wanted to see you again."

"It is nice to be remembered for oneself. Flattering, I suppose," he was smiling to himself. They danced on and he felt the contours of her body and smelt her perfume and remembered the first time and guessed he would have no problems . . .

"Come on," she said when the music ended, "come on over and meet your benefactor."

"Why not . . . he ought to have some idea of the man his son will take after," he said, and followed her across to where the old man was sitting.

The introductions were so relaxed and the man's manners so pleasant that Paul could almost forget what he had been hired for. The conversation took on an almost surreal quality. Occasionally Paul would glance across to the

Baroness's place and find her eyes on his. She was smiling, amused, almost laughing, but not at him, he was sure.

"We've just come on from Paris," said the coffee planter.

"Oh, yes, Paul, it was lovely! Have you been to Paris?" Helga asked.

"Yes," he said. "I went there on . . . business. A handsome city but I found the people rather too Prussian for my liking."

"Oh, Paul!" she laughed.

"What d'you mean?" asked her husband.

"I mean that underneath the *gay Paree* bit, they are as calculating as we are . . . Actually they're worse because we are calculatingly correct while they are calculating just how much they can cheat you."

"You found that, did you?" asked the planter, leaning forward and very interested.

"I'm not sure . . ." said Paul. "If I say so, I must have done. It didn't matter about the cheating, of course – it wasn't me they were robbing. Anyway, I took it all as my own personal reparation."

"Paul," exclaimed Helga, "the thoughts and ideas you have these days!"

They danced some more and the husband seemed content to watch them. He did not know of, or did not care to think about their previous intimacy and his stake in the intimacy to come was too high for him to quibble.

"Strange," thought Paul, "that he is prepared to pay so much so his wife can cuckold him. She looks lovely, it's true, but no matter how much she's lied, surely he must know that she is nearly past the age of child bearing?"

He startled himself with his own thinking and nearly missed a step. Dancing was like driving a tram, you had to concentrate.

After another bottle of wine and more dancing, Helga decided it was nearly time for bed and the fertility rites and the conception. It was clear that she had prearranged the moment with her husband because he left them very easily and without embarrassment. They danced once more and Paul said he thought the old man must be rather nice.

"Nice, but very old," she said, clinging just a little too

tightly.

They left the bar and walked through the main hotel. The little gilded cage was waiting and they stepped in. The lift boy smiled without malice or envy and moved the arm and the lift rose up, up towards Helga's boudoir. In the lift, she put her arm through Paul's in a proprietorial fashion. She was paying, he didn't care.

They didn't speak as the lift went gracefully up. He tried to recall passion he had known with her. Passion of flesh, passion of temper. He couldn't recapture any of the sensations but he could remember his feelings of gratitude that afternoon in the cemetery. He felt well disposed towards her and patted the hand holding his arm. She smiled, sweetly, almost simperingly: "Paul," she said, and the voice was urgent enough to make the little lift boy's back go rigid as he responded to the animal notes in her call.

They walked along the thickly carpeted corridor and stopped in front of the door. She handed the key to Paul and he opened the door. He followed Helga in and found himself in a little vestibule which led into a huge bedroom. It was elegant of its period and entirely lined in pleated grey silk – voluptuous without being heavy handed.

Helga slipped from the dress she was wearing and from everything else and lay on the bed on the pink satin sheets. Her body was still beautiful and still desirable and Paul felt himself rising to the occasion. The memory links were strong but the training of the past few years was stronger. He took his clothes off gracefully and hung them with precision but without fuss over the clothes stand. His money, loose change, watch, he placed on the hollowed ledge.

She waited, too sophisticated to look impatient, too impatient to be able to hide her desire. He moved to the bed and lay beside her. While he looked into her eyes, his hand moved down her body. Over her breasts and down to her perfect belly and beyond.

"Paul, kiss me," she murmured. He kissed her, letting his lips rest gently on hers at first and then letting the kiss take the full weight of his body as he lowered himself from his elbow.

He lay alongside her, kissing her and looking at her face

while his slender fingers charted her body for his brain to recognise shoals and reefs and deep, warm water bays.

The excitement transmitted from his finger tips through the nerves in his arm to his brain and there translated into the recognition of fleshy pleasure was no longer enough. His eyes needed to see what his fingers could caress.

He took his lips from her open mouth and turned his head to look down the length of her curved white body. For a moment he felt an interest which he had not known for a very long time. It was a pity that she had wanted more than he had been prepared to give. Perhaps in time he would have become as violent in his lust for life as he used to be in his lust for her body. Anyway, here was a reprise of the situation.

Helga was ready for him and he was ready for her – with a vengeance. As he was turning his head back to hers, prior to a union, his eye registered a wedge of light on the ceiling. He raised himself slightly so that he could see over the end of the bed. There, sitting on the end of a bed in the open doorway which led to the adjoining bedroom, still immaculate, still clasping his cane in his hands, sat Helga's husband.

He was thoughtful and excited at the same time. His eyes protruded a little and his tongue brushed nervously over his top lip. He saw Paul looking at him and returned his gaze. Paul felt that he was so much part of the scene that he might as well be on the bed alongside them.

"Your husband's here," he whispered.

"I know," she answered.

"Well what's he doing there?"

"Dear Paul, he's paying. It's only right that he sees his money is spent on the man I said it would be."

"But does he have to watch? Now that he's seen me here, going this far, surely he can trust you not to sneak out and get served by a labourer?"

"Oh, Paul," she said, petulance and anger creeping into her voice: "What difference does it make?"

"It makes a great difference to me . . ." said Paul, looking down the length of his body where his interest was being sapped like a rich piece of vegetation is sucked dry by greenfly. "Yes, it makes a great deal of difference to me!"

He slid off the bed and started to dress. The husband sat and stared at him and Helga kept wailing his name.

"It's no good," he said.

He dressed quickly and deftly and in a few minutes, he was leaving the room looking as smart as when he walked in.

"Goodnight," he said.

"Paul!" she shouted after him. Her husband sat immobile till he had gone then he got up and walked across to the bed and silently shook his stick at his wife.

"What are you doing that for?" she asked. "It wasn't my fault ... You would sit there like a dried-up voyeur. Of course he wouldn't perform."

"He's a professional male whore. He should be able to perform under any circumstances," he growled.

"He's different," Helga shouted. "He's sensitive. He's not some roaring bull of a man."

"I suppose that means his underwear is made of silk and he will only accept money that has come straight off the printing press!"

* * * * *

EIGHTEEN

The invitation was for the reception only. Perhaps they thought he would be bored sitting through a nuptial mass for an hour or so; perhaps even they knew where the final line of good-taste had to be drawn.

A lot of his colleagues had also received invitations. They were asked because of their family connections. Eden Bar patrons got the message that it was not business as usual the coming Saturday.

Paul dressed carefully and wondered if the Prince had been happy for him to get his invite. Maybe he only wanted Cilly as an idea and the fact that she'd taken other lovers before him or that one of them was coming to his wedding reception did not bother him.

"We Princes have to be different," he'd said.

The taxi ride out to the Swanenwerder was very pleasant. Paul sat well back in his seat and watched the darkened city flow by. He felt elated and sad at the same time. He was sad to be finally losing all hope of Cilly but elated because now, perhaps, he could accept things as they were without a false, nagging hope. Maybe he would go to America.

As the taxi pulled off the road and on to the drive of the Prince's mansion, Paul saw that the whole place was *en fete*. All up and down the drive, parked on either side, there were vast limousines: white-wall tyred sedanca de villes like gangsters drove and stiff, formal carriages of the older aristocracy.

The house was a blaze of light and the sound of music and human noise filled the air. Champagne corks were popping like machine guns and there were screams of laughter from the young and sillier girls who were determined to be wicked tonight – if possible – with one of the Eden boys.

Paul paid off the taxi and walked up the steps. The major domo took his card and looked at it and pointed to a long line of people: "The Prince and Princess are receiving their guests in the long drawing room," he said.

Paul could see that most of the people lining up were of the older generation, the young ones were giving that a miss as being too frantically boring – but he wanted Cilly to know he was here and anyway, underneath it all, he was a very correct if somewhat rudderless Prussian.

The line shuffled forward and finally he reached the drawing room doors. The Prince was as tall and imposing as ever in a white brocade jacket. Cilly, he was surprised to see was wearing a very virginal, white wedding gown.

He looked at her for a little while before she finally saw him. She was still almost the same though a little of the Hollywood training had touched her and some of the cinema pertness clung on. But she was livelier and wickeder than celluloid could portray. She was animated even when she was shaking hands with an eighty-year-old remnant of a great Hanoverian family. It was in her and it gave Paul much cause for regret that he had lost her for ever.

She saw him between one handshake and another and her face lit up so much that the Prince saw and looked down the line. He knew at once that Paul was the cause of her joy. He smiled at Paul.

In the long drawing room, the line moved forward at a stately pace but in all the other rooms around came the noise of madcap revelry. Through the windows which led on to the terrace Paul could see people racing up and down. Footmen dodged between the guests carrying great silver trays of drinks and food, champagne in silver buckets, caviar in ice-encrusted crystal bowls. The atmosphere of richness was everywhere.

Standing on a table and as yet untouched there was a huge, tiered wedding cake which was a confectioner's dream of iced whorls and rosettes. It was much more Hollywood than German princeling.

The older people were swathed in tail coats and old Imperial orders, their women were walking yards of apricot and peach satin, pink organza and white tulle, be-ribboned, sashed with orders, topped with diamonds of ancient cut which were more a blur of light than a flash. The younger generation were all tuxedo'd and bare flesh. The smarter the dress and the more it cost, the less material there was to show for the money. The girls were sleekly, brilliantly bobbed, and their faces were all composed of huge mascara'd eyes and bright-red bowed lips. The older generation pretended not to notice the young, and the younger generation ignored the old.

At last Paul reached the receiving end of the line: "Lieutenant," said the Prince. "I'm delighted you could make it."

"Thank you, Prince," he said. "My congratulations." Cilly took his hand and stared into his eyes: "Paul," she said. "Paul."

"Hello, Cilly. My congratulations to you, as well."

"Well," said the Prince. "I imagine you're pretty tired of shaking hands by now, my dear ... Why don't you go off to some quiet place and relax ... There aren't many more people to come and I can receive them."

"Thank you, darling," she said, and already was moving away with Paul in tow before he had finished his charming, rehearsed speech.

Cilly led him through the chattering, glittering crowds till she found a quiet spot and sat down. He lowered himself beside her.

"I knew you'd come," she said simply.

"Did you?" he asked.

"Yes, you're like a comet that visits its star every two or three years."

"Every two or three light years – I've seen your film – twice," he said.

"Did you? ... Well, aren't you going to say something ...? Wish me well ...?" she sounded a little anxious.

"I wish you well both in your marriage and your career. There!"

"Paul, you aren't angry or hurt, are you?"

"Angry? Hurt? What about? Why?"

"About me marrying the Prince. It was always on the cards and you never asked me," she said.

"You never gave me the chance – even if I'd wanted to. Why did you run off like that...without even a word of goodbye?"

She made a face: "Paul, that's one of our rules. You never tell me anything and I never tell you. Anyway, I don't believe you would have asked me to marry you."

"I wanted to but you never gave me the chance."

"Oh, Paul, really!"

"How was Hollywood?"

"It's fantastic, wild, wonderful!"

He was a little disappointed to hear such enthusiasm: "Really?" he said.

"Yes!"

"How about the people? What are the people like?" He didn't really care what they were like.

"All over seven feet tall and all with two noses." She saw he wasn't listening and shook her head in disbelief: "Paul!" She grabbed him by the hand and dragged him up to his feet: "Let's get out of here," she said, and headed for the door. At that moment it opened and Captain Kraft came in. He was wearing a spanking new, full-length leather coat and he was bursting with confidence.

"Well," he said, looking at Paul and smiling slightly, "if it isn't the gigolo. How's business?"

"What ever are you doing at a function like this?" Paul asked. He was just a little too incredulous and Herman's self confidence sagged a little.

"The Party is moving up in the world, Lieutenant. People who matter are beginning to take us seriously . . . ah, hello, Prince. Congratulations!"

The Prince had come up behind them, still smiling.

"Hello," he said to Herman. "Having a good time? Are there enough pretty young girls here for you?"

He meant the question kindly but Herman was now even more huffy: "Yes, thank you Prince, though we Party officials have more serious things on our minds."

"Of course," said the Prince, and put his hand on Herman's shoulder to steer him away from Paul and Cilly: "By the way, there's one of the Party's leading men here from Munich. Have you met him? He has a strange name . . . begins with an 'H' if I remember . . ."

They strolled away from the young couple. In the other room, someone was playing the gramophone. The song was all the rage in Berlin and Paris though London was unaffected by it. The subject matter was love and money: "Let's dance," said Cilly.

They started dancing through the door into the room where the music was playing. Paul was humming, Cilly sang the words: "Just a *gigolo, dum de dum de dum* . . ."

"It's been a long time," said Paul.

"You're so much more interesting now."

Paul raised his eyebrows: "Why, Cilly?"

"Being a gigolo! It's fascinating being paid to do what other men actually pay for."

"Yes, though they pay to do it with women of their own choice."

"Well, you're my choice, darling," she said.

"It's a lovely idea, but I'm afraid it can't be thus tonight. I'm booked."

"But it's my wedding night and you'd make a beautiful present."

"Unfortunately I'm very expensive. Well outside the range of most pockets." The banter was becoming serious.

"Oh, I can afford you, my dear," she said.

"Can you indeed?" His voice was growing a little icy.

She took off her pearl necklace: "I think this would more than cover the cost," she said. "At least, it should be enough to pay for a couple of hours, even at the Baroness's prices!"

"Cilly, really!"

"You do want me, don't you?" she insisted.

"Yes, but . . ."

"Oh, come on!" she said, "Let's walk outside for a while, maybe the night will bring out the romantic side of your nature."

Paul thought of the Prince and he thought of Cilly and he weighed the decent thing against desire and felt, slightly sadly, that desire would probably win over decency given half a chance.

Herman wandered around the party feeling he should either be enjoying himself or roundly attacking the decadence surrounding him. He could not enjoy himself because he was ill at ease and he could not condemn the decadence because those enjoying it were of such a superior social status that he was too frightened to judge them openly.

Herman felt things strongly but never quite knew why.

Flashes of dull light inside his head told him that this was the new Germany and that the old had passed away along the Somme and would never come again. He was not happy with the new and longed for the Party to take control but then other dull flashes of insight let him see that the Party would use methods not quite decent by the old standards. It was very puzzling for him.

The man from Munich had not been impressed by Herman or his new leather coat: "Teach the Reds a lesson," he said, opaque eyes staring, small moustache bristling. "It only needs one good lesson to make the citizens of Berlin sit up and take notice."

Their footsteps led them away from the riotous noise coming from the house and towards the little gazebo. Lights from the house flooded down across the sweeping lawns but beyond the range of those lights, the garden was softly lit by paper Chinese lanterns. The pink and orange colours tinged Cilly's dress so that it stopped being quite so virginal. This encouraged Paul.

The gazebo was a pretty thing of cast iron and wood. Cilly led the way up the steps. Inside, what little light there was came in patterns through leaf-designed metal. It gave enough light to see by but not to distinguish a blush. Paul doubted that Cilly was blushing.

"Isn't this a sweet place?" she asked, lifting her dress. It was made up of a series of veils and reminded Paul of John the Baptist. He visualised his own head on a bloody silver salver but the sight of it in his mind's eye did not unduly impress him.

"Sweet," he said, mingling his hand with the veils and touching her flesh. She lifted her head slightly and he kissed her. She clung to him and they went through the ritual foreplay of love standing up.

The Prince and his older guests had been driven into a defensive position at the end of the long drawing room. Between them and the wild, abandoned, whirling younger members stood a thin line of defence of weary footmen. Their main redoubt was the great iced cake. Around the bottom of the cake, light mortars in the form of half finished cigarettes had landed.

"Such fun, such enthusiasm," someone was saying to the Prince, who nodded and smiled benignly the whole time.

Lothar and a group of Brownshirts in belted brown leather coats they had not attempted to remove, strode through a mass of pulsating young bodies. Their eyes were anxious but they exuded enough bad atmosphere to slightly dampen some of the more extravagant ebullience. They saw Herman standing alone like a melting rock in a moving sea. He still looked puzzled and depressed. They hurried over to him.

"The Reds are up to something," whispered Lothar.

It was not the news that Herman needed tonight: "What is it? Are there many of them?"

"Quite a few, Sir," said the Brownshirt. "They're massing over near Savignyplatz."

"How many men have we got at headquarters?" Herman asked.

"Not enough – we would have had more . . ."

"Yes, yes! Oh, God! Why tonight? Never mind, we've got to put on a good show. Teach those bastards a lesson."

"Couldn't we just ignore them for tonight? Leave it to the police?"

"No, we can't . . . Not possible . . . Munich's here . . . Come on!" Herman looked across the room and saw the Prince wave faintly to him. He gave a brave salute and left the room followed by his men and gusts of relieved laughter from the throng.

Passion had reached fever pitch and there was now nowhere to go but floorwards. As they moved down to the clean but hardly comfortable floorboards, Paul was glad that man had the naturally active role in love making. Their passion was strong and their desire burning but it was unfortunate that the climatic force should be reached in such discomfort.

"Cilly . . ." he said, when they had adjusted to the place. ". . . Are you alright?"

"Oh, yes, darling," she answered. He kissed her and tasted the little beads of sweat on her mouth.

It was strange that the great moments of his life were played out in awkward surroundings. He who was used to silk sheets had lost his virginity in a general's mausoleum and was now making love to the one real thing in his life and conscious only that his knees were rubbing roughly on unpolished wood.

"Is it alright?" he asked again. It would have to be. Nothing much could stop the course of events now.

"Oh darling!" she said, near to tears. "Darling!"

"Cilly!" The name became a word and the word became a roar and a flash. A feeling of triumph came over him again and just for the moment he felt he was a real man capable of making real decisions. "I'll do it now," he thought but even as he thought it, his body let him down and jumped the gun.

"Cilly!"

"Paul!"

"I love you!"

They clung together long after the passion had spent itself. They shifted slightly from time to time to ease an aching limb or start the blood flowing again where the circulation had been cut off but finally they had to get up.

They re-arranged themselves quickly, not looking at each other. As Paul put on his jacket, he felt the heavy string pearls in his pocket bump against his thigh: "Here," he said, handing them to her. "This is my wedding present to you."

"Paul," she said, taking the necklace and putting it on, "why don't you stay with me, just for tonight?" Their profiles were outlined in silver, like moonlit clouds.

"What about the Prince – your husband?" he asked.

"Oh, that doesn't matter."

"I see . . . And what happens tomorrow morning . . .? Will it be just like last time . . .? I awake with the dawn to find my lover gone . . .?

"I have to be up early . . . that's true . . . to start a film . . ."

"Yes, and after that film . . . what then . . .?"

"Back to Hollywood . . ." she said.

"Back to Hollywood . . ." he repeated.

"But I don't have to go . . . I don't have to do anything

unless you want me to. Paul . . . Paul! I know you love me . . . why won't you just stay with me?"

"I have my duties to do, you know."

"Duties!"

"Yes, well, they may seem a little strange – but I chose this way when I couldn't think of anything else to do and somehow I feel it has to go on like this."

"It doesn't have to go on like this. I'm rich, now . . ." she said, and he immediately picked her up.

"There you see? Didn't I say it would go on, with you or with many? And what about the Prince?"

"Oh, shit to the Prince!" she shouted.

"Cilly . . . From revolutionary to film star to princess . . . It's a fairy tale – but it's your fairy tale, not mine. I've made my many beds and I'm tied to them."

"But your heart," she said, close to tears. "You love me, think about that . . ."

"My heart . . . tell you what, my heart's always yours and any time you come back, just give von Semering a ring at the Eden. She'll fit you in with my heart if you give her enough warning."

He kissed her hand and turned to leave. In the faint light inside the gazebo he saw the glint of tears in her eyes and on her cheeks. It was no time to be moved and what was left of him was totally unmovable.

He walked back through the house and the party which was still going on. He did not see the Prince who was still in the long drawing room, his troops of the previous generation, fatigued by the noise of their offspring and too much rich food, were sadly depleted: his bodyguard of mercenaries in the form of footmen, listless and longing wearily for bed. He would have said good night, if he had seen him, but he did not – and he supposed the Prince would not take it amiss if he left without offering the courtesy.

In the hall, small groups were making a move to their cars and Paul asked for and was given a lift back into town. It was late, but the Eden Bar was still open: He thought he would go there for a last drink. The people in the car dropped him off and went on their way, baying and hooting like mad English huntsmen. He made his way on foot to his favourite and only place.

The bar seemed completely deserted. Klaus stood behind the bar, the only brightly lit spot, and waited for the customers who would not be arriving. The pianist tinkled idly and the melody came in sad snatches.

Paul sat at a table in the shadows and watched.

At first he thought that even the Baroness was missing but a moment or two later, her figure rose from the dark alcove and she walked over to the piano. As if on cue for a pre-arranged number, the pianist played the introduction to the song which was all the rage of Berlin and Paris but which London chose to ignore.

When he reached the verse, she began to sing:

'Just a gigolo
everywhere I go
people know the part I'm playing.
Paid for every dance,
selling each romance,
every night some heart betraying.
There will come a day,
youth will fade away
then what will they say about me?
When the end comes I know
they'll say just a gigolo,
as life goes on, without me'

She sang with great emotion and though he could not be sure that the blue eyes had picked him out in the gloom, Paul was sure she was singing for him.

"*I am a gigolo*," he thought. "In place of anything better to sell, I sell myself."

He got up and left the room.

He walked through the empty streets, his head bent and his hands in his pockets and tried to analyse his life. He did not notice that on street corners ahead of him, people were silently coming and going.

He thought that his life should have ended when the shell blew him into the white clouds. Maybe it had – but he had slipped through the fingers of the Great Reaper who could not see his falling body in all the smoke and debris.

He wouldn't call it a lease of life. Even the dullest life had some purpose and his had not. Across the road, ahead of him, a band of silent men in workers' overalls crossed silently. They were carrying rifles.

He might as well have died. He hadn't been much alive since then, and when he had been, it had only hurt.

He went under the underpass and made his way to a flight of stairs. Strangely lit, so he looked as if he were climbing to the stars. At the top, the dim lights reflected on the shiny leather coats of other armed men. He was in a tatty railway arch. Had he been a bottle here?

He supposed there must be some reason why a successful whore was admired while a successful gigolo was not. He couldn't for the life of him think what it was but it really wasn't very important . . .

The men at the top of the stairs dashed backwards as a band of workers appeared behind Paul. One of them fired at the retreating Brownshirts and the bullet ricochetted past Paul's head. He stopped for a moment to think about the meaning of that and could find none.

His mind turned to Cilly. Could she have been happy with him? He did seem rather negative at times – it would probably have irritated her no end. He walked on along the seedy, peeling tunnel and another bullet hit the wall beside him. Then an answering shot pierced his body and he was conscious of some surprise but no pain.

He tried to walk on and staggered and fell. The floor was not very clean or comfortable and the soft white clouds were above him. They should be underneath.

The Brownshirts began to creep back towards him and the Communists came up the stairs. Both sides stopped, eyeing each other, and Paul where he lay fallen.

"Is he one of ours?" a Brownshirt asked.

"I shouldn't think so, but he's not one of theirs, either. He's dressed up like somebody who's been to a party."

The Communists moved up to where Paul was lying and the Brownshirts closed in to prevent them taking the body.

The white clouds were getting denser but through them Paul could hear voices arguing over him the way voices never had before.

"He's ours!" somebody shouted.

"No he's not, you bastards, he's one of ours!"

"Then why did you shoot him?"

"I'm shot," thought Paul. "But I can't feel it. Oh, God, don't let me wake up in a French hospital again!"

He heard the sound of scuffling and the noises that schoolboys make when they are squaring up to each other. Then there were footsteps running down the stairs and then there was a voice he recognised.

"Well, well, well," said Herman. "So fate has brought you back to us after all?"

Paul tried to open his eyes and succeeded long enough to see Herman kneeling beside him and looking very solemn. He tried not to laugh. The white clouds were growing very thick.

Herman's voice was very thick, too. He was quoting something about unintentional heroes but Paul was very tired, now, and he gave one last little sigh of pleasure and went to sleep.

"He's gone," said Herman to his troops. "Pick him up carefully and take him to headquarters."

The black clouds turned white again Paul saw Mutti polishing the tiles in clouds of steam: "Mutti!" he called softly. At first she didn't hear: "Mutti," he spoke a little louder. She turned. She was puzzled: "Paul? Is that you? What a long time you've been away again." The white turned black and he gave one last start.

"He moved," said one of the men carrying him.

"That was just a nervous spasm," said Herman.

They dressed him in a smartly pressed Brownshirt uniform with the swastika armband, and laid him on a high bier against the wall. Over him hung a swastika banner.

Mutti came into the room with Aunt Hilda, pushing her husband in his wheelchair and stopped dead when she saw him.

"My son," she said, and her eyes filled with tears. Then she took in the uniform and the flag.

"Why is he dressed like that?" she asked. "He wasn't one

of you, was he?"

"He was," said Herman. "One of the best. One in a million." Mutti gave him a sideways look which made him feel uncomfortable and then dropped her gaze.

"Was it a bullet?" she asked.

"Through the heart," he said, proudly.

"Gustav," she whispered. "Did you hear that. It was a bullet. A hero's death."

The party turned to leave and as they did, the Colonel finally moved.

He turned his head right round so that he could see his son's body until they closed the doors to the room.

* * * * *